I Kissed Three Boys

ROYAL HAREM
BOOK ONE

LEXIE MIERS

Author note:

There is a 'fantastical' element to this otherwise contemporary romance.

I was inspired by a reader in a Reverse Harem group who put up a meme with the writing prompt:

"When you were seven, you held a fake wedding by the swings with a kid (or in this case- kids) you met at the park. You never saw your childhood 'spouse' again.
Today you received a letter summoning you to a foreign country... where your wedding to the heir to the throne twenty years ago is seen as valid."

I have also taken liberties with the laws and details of the country Lichtenstein 😊

I really hope you enjoy the first story in this royal harem series.

CHAPTER 1

Erin

When I was little, I had so many dreams about how amazing my life was going to be when I grew up. I'd have a great job—and a great guy, of course. Marriage, babies, maybe a nice house, too.

Life didn't deliver. Or at least, not so far. Things definitely hadn't turned out as I'd expected.

My twenty-seventh birthday was just around the corner, and I didn't have even *one* tick in *any* of those boxes. After four years together, my college boyfriend decided he was too young to be tied down and promptly disappeared. And, despite working my ass off for the past five years since then, I was nowhere near my dream job.

I'd managed to buy a cute, one-bedroom apartment that I was slowly decorating, but it wasn't exactly the house full of love and kids that I'd dreamt of. But then again, fairy tale dreams were written for kids, not adults. Right?

So, when an airplane ticket to some random European

country turned up in my mailbox, I assumed my parents had won the lottery and sent me a generous gift. They knew I'd always wanted to travel and hadn't been able to yet, so I figured this must be an early birthday present or something.

With the ticket clasped in my hand and my heart racing in my chest, I called my parents to thank them.

"Hey, Mom!" I said as soon as she picked up the phone. "Did you guys just send me a plane ticket?"

I stared at the papers in my hand. First class, too. They must have won *big*.

"Us?" Mom sounded as shocked as I was excited. "To where? Florida?"

They'd moved to Miami to be closer to the beach, and now that they were three states away, I rarely saw them anymore. As an only child, it kind of sucked.

"Uh... no." I stared at the very authentic-looking tickets and opened my laptop to do some research. "Maybe it was a prank or something."

Where the hell was Liechtenstein?

"Someone sent you a plane ticket? Is there a note or instructions or something?" she asked, like I was a regular surprise scavenger hunter or the oft recipient of charity plane tickets that came with instructions for what to do when I landed.

I peered inside the envelope the ticket had arrived in for probably the tenth time. "No. No note."

"Be careful, sweetheart," Mom cautioned, ever the wealth of wisdom. "There are a lot of scams around."

I rolled my eyes. "I know, Mom."

I was the one who'd grown up in a world with internet, smart phone hacks, and credit card fraud. My mom still had a DVD player because she refused to stream anything and Wi-Fi was a foreign concept, but I loved her more than anything.

Disheartened and more than a little confused, I changed the subject. "How's Dad?"

She went into detail about Dad's aching knees. They were weather-sensitive, could apparently predict rain better than the Channel 4 meteorologist, and I zoned out.

Had I missed a piece of the puzzle? Surely, there was more information in the envelope that I hadn't seen. I grabbed the ticket and looked over every corner of the paperwork. Nothing. The only clue was the time and date of the flight.

When Mom finished giving me all the pertinent information regarding Dad's ailments and then somehow switched subjects to and then finished telling me all about the people they'd made friends with down in Florida, I hung up and started pacing my apartment.

Would it be crazy to go to the airport and get on that plane? The answer was obvious. *Totally.* If I thought the ticket was sent to me by mistake, I wouldn't be so shaken, but the ticket had my name on it. It was definitely for me. In my name. Delivered to me. Which begged the question, *why?* Only one thing was truly clear. Whoever had sent it meant for me to appear in an obscure European country next week. And he or she finally realized what I'd known all along. I was meant to travel first class.

However, there were flaws to the first-class plan. Insurmountable flaws. Flaws that made this whole thing impossible. An impossibility of insurmountable...work. I had work. Things my employer paid me to do. Counted on me to do.

My cell phone rang, and I stared down at the screen displaying an overseas number. While I'd usually let an unknown caller go to voicemail, my gut told me to pick up.

"Hello, Erin speaking." This call felt different. It was my first from overseas.

"Hello, Erin. This is Henryk Gabelli."

His voice was insanely sexy—deep, masculine, exotic. He spoke the Queen's English but with an accent. The way he spoke —almost *too* proper—made me think he was some sort of lawyer or something.

"Hello there, Henryk," I said, grinning. A call from a sexy-voiced foreigner who knew my name. My normal Saturday was spinning into one mysterious day. "How can I help you?"

If this was a prank call or a sales pitch, a request from one of those foreign princes for my bank account number, I'd hang up. But for now, I perched on the edge of my kitchen stool, my stomach twisting with excitement.

"Well," he began. "You can confirm whether or not you received the plane ticket my steward sent you."

My jaw dropped. He had my attention. "Your steward?" *What the hell is a steward?*

"Yes. It seems we have a small problem that needs to be addressed." Interesting choice of the word *we.* "It's been explained that the only way to do so is to assure you have transportation to Liechtenstein so we can sort the issue."

"Hold on." I held the phone with my shoulder and opened my laptop, then put Mr. Fancy Pants on speaker and began typing. Where the hell was that country, exactly?

"Um... what's the problem you're referring to, Henryk?" I asked.

Such a cool name, and I was sure I'd heard it before, though for the life of me I couldn't figure out where.

Google flashed my results onto the screen. There were articles, a map, a Wikipedia entry. Just because I hadn't heard of Lichtenstein didn't mean no one else had.

Liechtenstein was a small European country full of castles, run by a noble family. Population only thirty-eight thousand people? That was tiny! A corner of New York. A neighborhood in Los Angeles. A piece of London.

"The problem is," Henryk began, then stopped and sighed heavily. "It's more suitable for you come over here and we can discuss it properly in person."

I narrowed my eyes even though he wasn't here to see it. "Look, buddy, I'm not going anywhere unless you tell me what's going on." I might have been excited by the idea of a paid-for European adventure, but I wasn't stupid.

Nothing "for free" came without major strings attached. Not in this world.

He heaved a sigh heavy enough for the weight of it to be heard halfway around the world. "Erin, do you remember a park with blue swings? In Washington? You were there on vacation with your parents, I believe."

Do I remember? My heart began to thump a little harder. Was this guy some sort of years-long stalker? How on earth did he know about a vacation I'd taken with my parents many moons ago? Correction. The blue swings—that day—it was *forever* ago.

"Yeah… what about it?" I asked, cautious as hell now.

"Do you also remember you married three boys that day because you couldn't decide who you liked better?" His tone was deeper with frustration, but his words took me back twenty years.

I froze then began to laugh. "Oh my God! Is that what this is about?" Henryk. A familiar name. Was this his roundabout way of looking me up after all this time?

I picked up the ticket that I'd set beside my laptop and looked at it. It appeared real enough. Had the airline logo. A seat number. Was stamped first-class. No one did paper tickets anymore, but wouldn't it have been quite the plot twist in this little mystery if it was real?

"I was one of those three boys. I had long brown hair back then." I'd been seven, but I had a vague recollection. So much time had gone by.

But then, I jumped to my feet as memories flashed across my brain. "Henryk! You had bright blue eyes and hair to your shoulders! You were so cute." That was probably too much information.

He sighed again, and I giggled. The situation wasn't as funny as it was entertaining, although I doubted he found it so. "Thank you, but that isn't the point of this phone call."

"Please tell me then, what *is* the point?" I asked, mimicking his pompous accent. "You didn't need to send me a fake plane ticket to reach out, you know."

"It's *not* fake." He sounded offended, every word sharper, and I almost laughed. Almost, but I was also processing. That ticket was *real*?

"And the *point*," he said, "is that, unfortunately, in my country, such a commitment, a promise, as it were... is legal."

I opened my mouth to respond, and for a few seconds, no words came out. Was he freaking serious? "We were seven years old!"

"I remember." His tone was dry, and I tried to picture him

now. Probably in a cardigan, with one of those fancy tobacco pipes, maybe a pocket watch. It was the image his tone inspired. "I imagine you are in shock. I was, as well. It is an unfortunate thing, but I need you to come to my country and legally release me from that bond."

I wanted to burst into hysterical laughter, but about the more I thought about it, the less funny this seemed. "You're serious, aren't you?"

"Deadly serious," he said, and if his words hadn't said it, his tone conveyed the depths of his solemnity.

"But I married all three of you that day!" So that made me a bigamist. Or a polygamist? I wasn't sure of the verbiage, nor did it matter. I threw my hands in the air. "You gave me a daisy, not a ring. It can't be legal. That's ridiculous!" Most ridiculous thing I'd ever heard.

This was bullshit. It had to be.

"Yes. That's the other problem," he said. I had to give him credit. From across the distance between his phone and mine, he'd managed to inspire my guilt reflex. I had married *three* boys that day. Caused this poor guy some sort of marriage problem. No telling what quandaries the others had found themselves in as a result of a game *when we were seven.*

I crossed my arms, my heart pounding hard. "What else is wrong?"

"Unfortunately, in this country, polygamy is legal. So, you'll have to sign a release form in relation to the other two boys as well as me."

"Yeah, fuck that." This time I cackled with laughter. "Okay, I appreciate a joke as much as the next girl, but you've got to be kidding me." I admired his dedication to it, though. To the thought that I'd been married since I was seven. I laughed and laughed until tears streamed down my face. He hadn't responded, so I said it again. "You can't be serious."

I sat down on my sofa, taking my phone with me. This had to be one of those candid camera jokes.

"Their names are Silas and Viktor, and they're being located as we speak." Now that he'd said the names, even more memories came pouring back. The daisies we'd picked, probably illegally, from the park. The solemn expressions on our faces as we swore our vows to one another. *Jesus.*

"Hopefully, we four can meet once more next weekend, sign our releases, and then never see each other again," Henryk said as if he were troubled by the whole thing.

I frowned. For a guy who was sending out free flights to his tiny little country, he was certainly in a big hurry to be rid of us.

"What's the rush, Henryk? Getting married?"

"Unfortunately, I am." He said it as if he had just been sentenced to life in prison.

My mouth dropped open. Well, that explained it. "Oh. Okay." The little girl in me who vividly remembered his bright blue eyes was jealous. The grown woman realized that was silly.

"It is an arranged marriage, not a love match." Well, that explained the dour tone. Pompous and dour still somehow managed to sound attractive.

But I got the feeling he didn't talk to Americans very often. "Erin, I am asking you... please, come. We are happy to compensate you for your time, of course. Perhaps a vacation after our business is concluded."

I frowned. I didn't remember the boy in the park being rich. "That's generous." What if he was some super rich drug lord, luring me to his country? I'd been watching a lot of streaming TV and it seemed like everyone was involved in a cartel these days. I didn't know Lichtenstein's economy, but I needed to know my involvement was with someone who didn't shoot first and snort questions later. "How can you afford that kind of thing?"

"I just can." Vague. I was about to say no, but he added, "So please, will you come?" It was just desperate enough to convince me, He certainly didn't sound like El Diablo.

I glanced down at the first-class ticket. Maybe he could afford it. And honestly, it was a free trip to a country I hadn't even known existed before and looked quite wealthy. "I'll have to speak to my boss first."

"Of course. But that is excellent news." Happiness—a chuckle —accompanied the words. Happiness or relief. "I look forward to meeting you again soon. My steward will send someone to meet you at the airport, and once we sign the releases, we can put all this mess behind us."

"Okay," I agreed, feeling strangely numb. *Mess?* That was a bit harsh to describe an innocent game of children. We'd been role-playing, pretending to be adults, nothing more. But I didn't comment further and it wouldn't have mattered if I had.

"Goodbye." Henryk abruptly hung up, and I sat on my sofa, dumbfounded.

At least today I couldn't say my life was boring.

CHAPTER 2

Erin

I worked for a marketing company and it was February, in a down time, of sorts. So, it might have been more than luck on my side when I walked into his office to ask my boss for two weeks off, especially since it was such short notice. He agreed that I could have the time, though the way he only half-smiled when he said it made me feel like I might not have a job to come back to.

Perhaps it wasn't good luck at all. Could've just been a squirrelly little man looking for an easy mark for downsizing. But I wasn't going to worry about that yet. I had enough on my plate.

Liechtenstein was north and east compared to South Carolina. And the internet said the average temperature wasn't much cooler than home. Probably wouldn't drop to freezing, but I wasn't taking chances.

And I didn't have a lot of cold weather clothes, so I decided a shopping spree was in order. I called my best friend, Bree, and she met me in one of the local stores I frequented on a regular basis.

"I can't believe you're just up and going to Europe. And without me no less," she lamented, shaking her head as we walked through Carolina Apparel.

"Well, if you have the money for a ticket, come with me," I told her. I had savings too, so if we needed to pay for some sort of accommodation upgrade, I was all for it. "I'd love the company."

Bree sighed and shook her head. "I can't. There's no way I'd get the time off work that quickly."

I rolled my eyes. "Yeah. I know."

Bree was the executive assistant to some bigwig in a finance firm. She had to give him six months' notice for a sick day. The money was good, though.

"Explain this whole thing to me again," Bree said, holding a white shirt with cold shoulders and long sleeves up against me. "What exactly is going to happen when you arrive in some foreign country that you never planned to visit? You could get kidnapped and sold into a human trafficking ring. You know that, right?"

"Liechtenstein isn't exactly known for human trafficking, Bree." Certainly not more than they were known for their cartels. I'd done some research, and though there were definitely some risks. I'd looked up the safest ways to travel and I'd be checking in with people back home every day. I had a plan.

"Then what happens?" she asked again. "You get there, see the rich boy ticket buyer and what?"

I selected a wool sweater and some thick socks and put them on the pile of clothes I was buying. "Henryk's steward called last night and gave me all the details."

Now that had been an experience. The steward was a strange man with an even thicker accent than Henryk's. All posh and haughty. I hoped the rest of Europe wouldn't be like that too. If it was, I'd spend the whole trip rolling my eyes at everyone.

Bree grimaced, with a look that reminded me of the same uncertainty I'd experienced when I heard that phrase. "What the hell's a steward?"

"I know, right? I think it's some sort of butler or servant for a rich family." A valet for a man. A maid for a woman. Rich.

Bree's mouth fell open. "Wow."

"Yeah. Well, anyway, the steward guy called. His name is Francis or something. Anyway, he said he would send someone to collect me from the airport, and then I'd meet Henryk and the other two guys at Henryk's apartment, sign whatever I need to sign, and then we'd be done." And my first "marriage" would be no more than a vague memory from days gone by.

Such a weird concept. I still couldn't fathom that a bunch of kids playing wedding with daisy chains could actually be legal. There was no license. No witnesses. Well, except each other. A marriage like this certainly wasn't legal in the United States.

Bree grinned at me. "So, your guy's servant is gonna send more servants to annul your play wedding?"

I laughed at the very idea of having such a chain of command beneath me. "Yeah, I guess so."

Bree picked up a pair of jeans. "Oh, these are cute. Go try them on."

I grabbed them and checked the size. "I'm not a size six, Bree, but they're cute. Grab a size ten."

Bree didn't argue, just threw me the jeans and we headed to the changing rooms. They fit great but were loose at the waist, which was often my problem. I had a small waist, but thick thighs and hips.

Dresses looked fine on me, but jeans weren't so easy to fit.

"You nailed it," I said to my friend. "These are great."

"I'll get the other stuff," she called to me. "Try on some of the sweaters, too."

I waited for her to bring me more clothes and went over the last day in my head for the hundredth time. I was going to Europe to sign away a marriage that, to me, was just ludicrous. Even if there was some sort of law in the words of a child's promise to another child, surely being seven years old should make anything about that situation null and void?

She flicked a pink sweater over the door, and I dragged it down and brushed my hands over the delightful fabric. "This is so soft."

I put the sweater to my face for a moment, before pulling it on. Another piece that fit perfectly over my big boobs.

Awesome.

"I don't get why he's doing this," Bree mused, standing outside the changing room door. "Why not just leave it?"

I grinned as I pulled a sweater up over my head and threw it onto the *maybe* pile. "He's getting married!"

And our daisy chain child wedding somehow stood in the way of his adult, legal wedding.

"Married?"

I actually laughed this time. "The way he said it, I don't think he even knows who his bride is. He said it's some sort of arranged marriage."

Another concept that was incredibly foreign to me. Marry someone I'd never met? Someone my parents had chosen for me? I could picture the pocket protectors and wire rimmed glasses. The family car and Sunday night bowling league. Uh... no, thank you.

I reached for a black sweater and tried it on. It was too tight at my hips and the arms were too long as well.

"Arranged marriage? Do people still do those?" Bree called through the door.

I shrugged. *Nope, definitely don't like the black. Now for the turquoise one...* "In some parts of the world, I guess. But honestly, I have no idea. It sounds totally medieval, doesn't it!"

Bree chuckled on the other side of the door. "Medieval is right! Have you even googled Liechtenstein? It's full of castles and all things ancient."

I opened the door, bringing with me the clothes I had decided to buy. "Yeah, I did, but I won't be staying there long. Henryk said they'll set me up with some travel plans after that. I thought I'd go to France or Spain or somewhere more touristy."

I hadn't been on a vacation in years, and certainly I'd never been to Europe. The small number of times I took off work were used to catch up with friends, renovate my old apartment, or visit my parents in Miami.

"It's still shouting *scam*, Erin. You know that, right?"

I sighed and worked my way around the racks of clothes to the counter. Then I put the items down for the girl to ring up. "There's only one way he knew about that park, Bree, and what happened that day. And that was because he was there."

The details were too perfect. Who else would have known what I did as a child on vacation twenty years ago? With that fact paired with the first-class plane ticket, I was starting to believe in miracles.

Bree grinned at me, her eyes sparkling with mischief. "How come you never told me that story?"

"I was seven. I haven't thought about it in years." I paid for the clothes and took my bags off the counter. "Thanks."

"Lunch?" Bree pointed toward the street where a plethora of cafes and restaurants sat.

I nodded. "Yeah. I'm starving."

We made our way to the closest cafe, ordered some lunch, then Bree turned to me again. "Tell me the story. How on earth did you marry three boys in a park in one day?"

I covered my face with my hands. "It wasn't just in one day, it was all at once."

"Fine." I lowered my hands again and picked up my glass of water, taking a sip while I gathered my thoughts. "My parents took me to Washington DC to see the White House and all that stuff one summer."

"Yeah?" Her mouth lifted into a grin and her eyes lit up.

"And while we were there, I played in this park near our hotel. Every day, these same two little boys, Silas and Viktor, played there too. They were so cute and nice." I smiled at the memory. Unlike other boys I'd met, they didn't try to knock me over or say I had girl germs.

"Then how did Henry come into it?" She was so interested in this whole story. But life in general interested Bree. She loved new experiences, whether they were hers or mine.

"Henryk," I corrected, taking my iced coffee from the waiter.

Bree narrowed her eyes, fake angry. "Fine. How did *Henryk* come into all of that?"

I took a sip of my drink and licked the cream off a corner of my lip. My mind pulled up an old memory of the quiet little boy with big, blue eyes. He'd been so gorgeous, even to my seven-year-old self.

"Well, on the day before we were leaving to come home, Henryk came to the park. He didn't seem to want to play and just stood in the corner of the playground, watching us all." I could picture him, close my eyes and still see him.

Bree laughed at me. "And you went and invited him to play, didn't you? You can't stand seeing anyone miss out."

I shrugged. I'd always hated bullies and hated seeing kids who were shy or different be ignored.

"Yeah, well, I got him to come play with the three of us, and then he told me I was the nicest girl he'd ever met, and he wanted to marry me." I smiled at the memory. Crying shame no one else had felt that way since then.

"So, you 'married' him?" Bree asked, using her hands to bunny-ear the word *married*.

I laughed. "Yeah." And it had been sweet, although I doubted I appreciated exactly how much until now.

"So how did the other guys come into it?"

I snorted. "Well, Viktor and Silas weren't about to miss out, and they said they wanted to marry me, too. So, we did."

I shrugged and thanked the waiter for my salad, then I picked up my fork and stabbed a small, sliced piece of chicken.

Bree took a sip of her cappuccino and sighed. "It's like some sort of fairy tale."

"And now I'm still married to all of them," I said, "Totally unbelievable and insane."

She laughed and we finished lunch. I was officially leaving for Europe tomorrow, and since I had plenty of warm clothes, a plane ticket and a passport, there was nothing stopping me now.

Erin

Flying first class was like a dream come true. The direct flight was just under twelve hours, and I didn't want to close my eyes for a single second. A flight attendant with bouffant hair and a scarf tired around her polo collar brought me alcohol and a plate of delicious food, and in the end, I ended up sleeping for a few hours. Not because I wanted to, but because the sleep pods were so comfortable, it just didn't feel right staying awake.

When I woke, rested and slightly tipsy, we were landing. My stomach was jumpy and anxious, yet excited, and a squeal built in my throat.

The first-class passengers were allowed to disembark first, but I didn't really want to do that. I shimmied down in my seat and looked around, watching everyone else leave.

I liked the idea of not having to push and wait in line with the rest of those in coach, but I also didn't really want this amazing experience to end.

"Would you like help with your bags?" a different flight attendant asked, standing beside my little sleep pod.

I sighed and grabbed my satchel, throwing it over my shoulder. "No, I'm fine. Time to face the music, I guess."

No one really understood what I meant, but I grinned at her and wove my way down the aisle, then out into the airport terminal. Up ahead of me, there was a young man in a suit, holding a white sign.

Erin Wright.

I pasted on a grin as I stepped up in front of the "servant" Henryk's steward had sent to collect me. "Hey. I'm Erin."

Much to my surprise, the guy's face lit up, and that was when I noticed the hint of black eye liner around his big blue eyes. "Hello, Erin. I'm Raymond."

"Hi, Raymond," I returned, sticking out my hand to shake his. "Nice to meet you. Can I call you Ray? You can call me Erin." If he called me Ms. Wright, I wouldn't know to answer anyway.

Ray glanced down and then shook my hand. He smiled as his warm palm slid against mine. "You are going to be a breath of fresh air around here." His accent wasn't English, but I couldn't place it. I guessed it would be German.

"Around the airport?" I asked.

Ray ignored my question and waved his other hand. "Luggage claim tickets, please."

I handed them over and followed him to the carousel, admiring Ray's fitted suit and gelled hair. This was a man who had style on top of swagger and some more style just because.

"So, tell me, Ray, what exactly do you do for Henryk?" I watched his shoulders from behind. They were broad but not too broad, and his hair hung over his collar just enough.

He grabbed my first suitcase and turned to raise an eyebrow at me. "Why do you ask?"

Did I dare say that he looked like someone's personal shopper?

"Uh..." I didn't dare.

Ray chuckled as he grabbed my second suitcase. "Is this everything?"

"Yeah, that's it." Two suitcases might've seemed excessive for a two-day trip, but it wasn't nearly enough for the couple week vacay I was planning for after.

He took my bags, and we made our way through the airport to a waiting, chauffeur-driven stretch limousine. The windows were tinted and there were about three miles between the back door and the front.

"Whoa. Fancy."

Ray laughed louder this time as he loaded my bags in the trunk, then came back to open the car door for me. "Hop in, Miss Wright."

I rolled my eyes at him. "It's Erin."

His eyes sparkled in amusement. "All right, Miss *Erin*."

Miss Erin. It sounded funny. "You don't meet many Americans, do you?"

He shook his head and waved me inside the car.

I sighed. "Fine."

Holy shit. This thing was amazing. Leather seats. Sunroof. A mini fridge with soda and bottled water.

Ray climbed in the front with the driver and shut his door.

"Um... you're seriously gonna leave me back here, like you're driving Miss Daisy or something?" I had no idea if he understood the reference, but Jessica Tandy was an international treasure in my book, so if he didn't know, I would introduce him.

He turned and looked over the seats separating us. "It's proper. Now, we're to meet His... Henryk..." He stumbled when he referred to Henry. Strange.

I frowned. I knew Henryk was rich, but his? His what? His Royal Highness? His Honor? Another plot twist in the Mystery of Lichtenstein and the wild Wedding of four seven-year-olds.

I opened my mouth to ask what the *His* referenced, but Ray spoke over the top of the silence. "At his city apartment. It's only ten minutes' drive, so please, enjoy the views, and we'll be there shortly."

Ray slid a glass panel up behind him, effectively shutting off communication between us, then he turned so I couldn't even wave at him to ask any more questions.

I glared at the back of his head and by the set of his shoulders, I was pretty sure he could tell. But I didn't have much of a choice, so I pulled out my cell phone and shot off some text messages to my parents and Bree.

Hi, everyone. I'm here and in one piece. Flight was great. Chat soon.

Mom sent back a message. *Have fun. Love you.*

Bree was a bit more erratic. *OMG! You're still alive! It is you, right?*

I giggled. *Yeah, it's me.*

Prove it.

"Oh my God." I laughed at her. I could've sent a photo, but she would think it was under duress.

When I divorce all three of my husbands, I'll send you another text.

That was enough for now.

LOL. And pics! I want LOTS of pics.

Of course, she did, and of course I would send them. *Deal.*

I exhaled slowly and the tightness in my chest eased as I stared out the window. "Wow." Lush, green landscape blew past us. We were still in the city but there were beautiful old buildings everywhere.

I shivered and ran my hands over my arms. There were touches of snow on the tallest buildings and decorating some of the window trims. I needed to put on more clothes when we got out of the car. I was dressed for the excessively warm, almost spring, in South Carolina that had been when I left.

When the vehicle pulled up in front of a large, modern building, I was almost disappointed. Now we just looked like we were in New York or somewhere almost familiar. I wished he would've been staying at one of those period places. I would've loved to explore a castle.

Maybe Ray could point me in the direction of the nearest one, and I could check it out before I headed to Spain.

The door opened and there was Ray, grinning down at me. "Do you have something warmer to wear?"

I nodded. "Yeah, I do. Let me just grab it out of my suitcase."

When I climbed out, Ray shut the door behind me. "You don't need it now. We'll go straight into the hotel, but I was just inquiring, if you're staying in Liechtenstein."

I shivered, grabbed my satchel, and hurried for the glass double doors at the entrance to the hotel. "I'm not staying. I'm heading to Spain as soon as possible."

To the sun, the cocktails, and the beaches.

I burst through the doors and a burst of warmth caressed my skin. Shivering again, I sighed at the same time. "God, that's better."

Ray came in behind me and instantly he stiffened. He straightened his jacket and stood taller.

I pressed my lips together. It wouldn't do to alienate the one person I knew in this country. "Everything okay, Ray?"

He didn't rise to my bait, instead nodded to the bank of elevators. "This way, Miss Erin."

I didn't mention his incorrect use of my name. Instead, I walked over to the elevator and pushed the call button. "Which floor?" I asked as we stepped into the car.

Ray took a card out of his pocket and swiped the reader. "The penthouse."

The elevator started moving, and I watched the numbers climb like I'd never seen numbers go so high, but there were only 18 floors plus PH—which I assumed meant penthouse. "Of course. He's rich. That makes sense." I murmured the words almost to myself, but Ray nodded ever so slightly.

The inner nervousness I'd been ignoring was now bubbling just beneath the surface. It wasn't that I was meeting my husband for the first time in years. It was that I was seeing *Henryk* again after all this time. And it was both exciting and terrifying.

I wondered if he would recognize me or if I would recognize him. We'd been so young back then. Had that gorgeous, serious little boy, grown into an equally serious, and also gorgeous man?

I took out my phone and shot Bree another message. It calmed me to put my troubles into words.

In the hotel elevator. Gonna meet Henryk in a minute.

The doors opened and I managed to see Bree's response before I disembarked.

If he's really, really rich, find out if he has a brother. Younger or older, I'm not picky.

My laugh died on my lips as I stepped out of the elevator and right into the largest, grandest apartment I'd ever seen. The ceilings were at least twenty feet high and there was a marble foyer. Columns. Floor-to-ceiling windows with long, billowing curtains. This place was opulent and white. So much white. I looked around, smiling, ready to run in and jump on the sofa in what I thought was my hotel room. I laughed, delighted by Henryk's choice of my accommodations.

And that was how I saw Henryk again for the first time. Giggling like a schoolgirl with my phone clutched in my hand.

Holy hell.

No. Holy shit.

No. Holy fuck.

My jaw dropped. He wasn't just gorgeous, he was *stunning*. The long hair was gone, cut closer these days, but the eyes were still so blue I could see them from across the room. I could see them while he was backlit by the fire he was standing in front of. They were the sky after the storm. His jaw was wide his legs long, his shoulders broad. But there was no doubt this was the same boy I'd "married" back on that playground in DC. And he was staring at me.

"Oh my God," I whispered, then covered my mouth with my fingertips. "This is so surreal."

Henryk walked forward, no sign of a smile or a welcome, but his eyes blazed hot and intense.

He inclined his head with what I assumed was supposed to be a greeting, but there was still no smile. "Erin. So good of you to come all this way."

He was like one of those chocolate eggs, so fragile and yummy and perfect. Perfectly perfect.

I rushed forward and hugged him, squeezing like we were old friends. And maybe we were. We were married after all, and I'd flown across an ocean and part of Europe to get here. If I wasn't a friend or some form of a friend, I wouldn't have come.

But this was such a strange moment, and with the hug, I took it to a whole other level. But when was I ever going to get to hug my pretend husband again?

It took a good ten seconds, ten awkward seconds by the way, before he patted my back just a little, before putting his arms down and straightening his body.

"Thank you for inviting me," I said. I sounded formal, but maybe because we hadn't said hello. We hadn't small talked or chit chatted and there wasn't a kind look between us. So with the exception of my hug, this was wholly a formal moment.

When I stepped away, he straightened even more, the same as Ray had. Were all these guys military trained?

"We're just waiting on the other two, and once they're here, we'll proceed." Henryk held out his hand, and I looked at it for a second. I didn't know what he wanted or what he was doing, but I laid mine in his and absorbed the tingles into my skin. Or maybe they started there, I didn't know. But they were wholly enjoyable. Even though I had no idea where he was taking me.

But he led me to gorgeous leather couches. "Please, sit. Do you need anything after your flight? A beverage? Something to eat?"

I sat down and ran my hands over the leather. It was like butter, smooth and cool. I looked up at him and smiled. "No. I'm fine, thank you."

A phone rang and Henryk tilted his head and pulled his lower lip between his teeth. "Excuse me." He headed over to the phone to pick it up.

Henryk's side of the conversation was in German, the primary language of Lichtenstein, according to Google.

While he took his call, I glanced around the room, my heart beating a little too fast. The designer had used gold accents and plush carpet and bright lights to infuse decadence into the décor. It certainly wasn't the sordid human trafficking scenario that Bree had conjured up.

When Henryk hung up the phone, I stole another glance at him. Which was a mistake of course, because every time I looked his way, my stomach twisted, and heat poured through me.

He was way too attractive.

His brow furrowed and I curled my fingers into a fist against the ridiculous urge to smooth the lines away. "Are you all right?"

"The plane delivering Viktor and Silas has been delayed and they won't be here until tomorrow." He spoke as if this was done purposefully to prolong the amount of time he had to spend with me. I didn't want to be offended. Unfortunately, I was.

I shrugged like I wasn't. "I'll find a hotel and just stay there for the night."

Tomorrow was another day. A big one. And I was going to see all of my "husbands" again. A week ago, I'd been lamenting the lack of excitement in my life, and now I was a polygamist, divorcing three men at once. If nothing else, I had a great new party story. Plus, I had a stamp in my passport. Finally.

Henryk sighed again. This was a man who, without saying a word, could make it sound as if the weight of the world rested solely on his shoulders. "I'm sorry, but I have commitments tomorrow that I simply can't reschedule. You can come back to the Vaduz with me tonight, and then we will have Silas and Viktor meet us there tomorrow." When I stared at him blankly, more concerned about the details now. The delay of the others' arrival was convenient. I had no idea where or what Vaduz was or why I would go there rather than to a hotel. What commitments were so important he couldn't reschedule to secure his divorce? "Vaduz Castle. It's the home of the royal family."

My mouth dropped open. "Did you just say castle?" And more than that, *Royal family?*

CHAPTER 4
Henryk

I'd promised my steward and my parents that I would *not* reveal my true position at the castle to Erin, but lying about it was not in my nature. It went against the grain to be dishonest at all, even more so to lie about who I was.

Erin was so much more beautiful in real life than in her photos. So lively, happy, and she'd actually made the trip. That meant something, though I didn't know what. All I knew for certain was that I wanted to wrap her up and take her home with me, just so she could shine some light into my gray and regimented life.

I cleared my throat, pushing such ridiculous thoughts from my mind. There was no time for such frivolity. No time to for consideration of wrapping her in anything or having her brightening anything. I had responsibilities and I couldn't believe this marital glitch was now continuing even longer, thanks to a commercial airline cock-up.

The only silver lining to having to wait for Viktor and Silas was that it gave me time to spend with Erin.

"Yes, I live in a royal castle," I said, answering the question she'd asked and ignoring the one she hadn't. For all I cared, she could think I was a servant. Last thing I needed was a greedy wife I didn't know wanting her Princess Diana moment.

Her eyes lit up. "Oh, really? Well, that would be awesome. I'd love to see it before I head off again." And suddenly, her American was on full display. She spoke like there was a premium on how many words she could say before she had to take a breath. "Can I talk to Francis while I'm there about my plans? He said he'd help me book some backpackers' place or something."

Backpackers? Ah... I don't think so.

Instead of voicing my thoughts, I smiled at her and said, "Francis will book everything for you this evening if you'd like."

She was studying me in a way that felt unfamiliar these days. No one looked at me anymore. Not the way she did. And she stared into my eyes when we spoke, also something no one did anymore. And she was all bright and bubbly, with no underlying nervousness or worry.

Everyone around me was always stiff and uncomfortable. They rarely looked me in the face, to the point that most of the time I didn't even feel like a real person—to them, or to myself.

Erin's openness was unexpectedly refreshing.

"That would be great." She beamed, and then tilted her head so that the light caught her eyes in a way that made them seem to glow and cast a halo at the top of her head. She was beautiful, as much as I remembered that little playground girl. And I had most definitely remembered her over the years. "Are we heading there now?"

I nodded because I couldn't find my voice for a second. "May as well." No point hanging around for a meeting that wasn't going to happen today. Not when two of the participants weren't even in the country. "I need a moment to pack up." I looked at her and waited for her to move. She did not. "Maybe you would like to freshen up?"

"Do I not look fresh?" Her brow pinched and she pushed her hand into her hair. She set her bag down on the leather sofa, breathed a whistling breath in through her nose then turned to me. "Could I use the restroom quickly?"

"Yes, of course. It's just down the hall on the right." I pointed her in the direction she needed, and with another of those wide smiles—the same ones from back then, and I liked it as much now—she headed off.

I watched her walk away. She had a sway to her hips that was as intoxicating as it was hypnotic to watch. She was curved and rounded, firm in plane and soft in curve. I couldn't look away.

"Sire." My security man Gerald's voice drew my attention away from the loveliness of Erin's form. "Do you wish to take your guest home with you?"

I turned to Gerald. Hardly ever noticed he was in the room because he stayed in corners and shadows nearby, ready to pounce if necessary, but generally unseen. When he did make his presence known, I liked to look at him while he spoke. "It wasn't the original plan, but I don't have any other option now."

The meetings I had scheduled at the palace tomorrow morning were a matter of public safety. I had no choice but to attend.

Which meant that my gamble had not paid off. I'd hoped I could sneak into the city, meet with Erin, Silas and Viktor, keeping this quiet. I'd be free of everything but the memory of this mistake and no one but those directly involved would be any the wiser. But... no. Fate apparently had an ironic sense of humor.

"As you wish." Gerald inclined his head. "We'll depart straight away."

He swept away and gathered the rest of his staff to provide instructions.

I packed up my computer and all the paperwork I'd brought with me. Divorce papers, times five. Who would've ever thought I would need four copies and a spare to be free enough to marry a woman I'd met once and had no real desire to meet again?

When Erin came back, she looked fresh and shimmering. "Are we leaving soon?" One of the things I loved about her, aside from her shiny auburn hair and those gray eyes was her voice. It was sultry and made me think of night and all the things I wanted from her, with her... Things I could never have.

I shook my head and picked up my briefcase. "Yes. We can walk down now if you like."

"Awesome." She beamed and I caught a glimpse from the corner of my eye as she fell into step alongside me. "Am I riding with you? I'd love to catch up on what you've been up to over the past fifteen years." I couldn't tell if she was teasing me or if she was serious. "I'm curious."

"Of course." I smiled politely, though I had no idea what to tell her.

We took the private elevator down to the ground level, where Gerald and his team escorted us outside into a waiting car.

"Ooh, this is so fancy!" Erin gushed, sliding into the stretch town car. "How far away is your... place? Your *castle*?" She said it like it was a disease and I had to admit that she was the first woman who'd ever said it like it was a bad thing to live in one of the hundred Lichtenstein castles. Not that I pulled or played that card often. There were women. Not a lot but enough to know that a castle wasn't a deterrent. Not a turn-off. Hell, at nineteen it had been a bonus.

Unfortunately, it wasn't far at all. For some reason, I found myself wanting to spend more time with Erin. As soon as we arrived, she would be whisked away to her guest quarters, and I wouldn't have the pleasure of those blinding smiles of hers any longer. They were the kind of smiles that made a man want and need and yearn. *I* yearned.

"About fifteen minutes," I told her. The castle sat upon a hilltop staring down over the city.

"Oh, great." She yawned loudly, lifting her hand to cover her mouth. "Sorry."

"*I'm* sorry. You must be tired." Jetlag was a real thing. She'd flown across a couple time zones.

She nodded. "I am. I didn't get much sleep on the plane. I was far too excited."

I couldn't help the smile. Her enthusiasm was infectious, and I couldn't stop watching her. She was spirited, oohing and aahing, finding delight in every single flower alongside of the rode—the wild ones left over from the winter—and mountain peaks on our way. I smiled and watched her because I couldn't stop smiling and I couldn't stop watching.

Too soon we turned into the castle grounds and the car sped up the drive to the gate.

Erin slid to the edge of the seat and stared out through the heavily tinted windows. "*This* is your home? Are you serious?"

She turned to stare at me with wide, shocked eyes.

I shrugged. "Yes. I live here." Most of the time. When I wasn't traveling or spending time in one of the other three castles my family owned in Liechtenstein.

We pulled up in front of the main entrance and a footman scurried over to open the vehicle door. His brow narrowed then his eyes went wide. He'd obviously not expected to find a woman, because I'd only left a couple hours ago and even for a prince, that would've been quick work. But he composed himself and offered his hand. "Miss."

She nodded and slipped her hand over his—lucky bastard—then swung her legs out of the vehicle. "Thank you." When she stood, she smiled at Oscar. "Hello, I'm Erin." He nodded and stepped back as I came around the car from the other side.

I took a shallow breath and shook my head. Bringing her here was wrong. A bad choice. But I ignored my instinct to send her straight to the nearest hotel and let her cool her heels until Silas and Viktor arrived. I supposed she could've signed before they arrived and been on her way, but I didn't make the offer. There was probably a subconscious reason.

"Erin will be staying in one of the guest rooms tonight, Oscar. Please inform the staff and make sure she's comfortable." This time, I was the one who threw him off. A guest room was hardly consistent when I was involved with a beautiful woman.

"Where are you going?" Erin asked before rushing over to grab her baggage out of the car.

"One of the house staff will carry those in for you," I told her as she hoisted her suitcases out of the trunk, one after the other, much to the dismay of my driver, who had tried to get there before her and failed.

"Oh, I'm fine. It's only one case, and a small bag, really." She fluttered her hands at the servants to send them away, then walked back over to me. "I'm ready. Where's Ray?"

She glanced around as if she expected that just by saying his name, he would appear, but even I didn't have that power. He hadn't been impressed when I'd assigned him the task of picking Erin up from the airport, but I needed her delivered safely and without mishap.

I tilted my head and considered her in the direct sunlight. She was stunning in any light. I didn't think the sun could make her more so, but I was wrong. "He was traveling in another car." My voice was thick, my body tight.

She nodded. "He was nice." And that was all she said, but I had a feeling she wanted to say more. I tilted my head and waited, but no further conversation ensued, so I turned to go up the stairs. But I stopped before I made even one step up.

"Nice?" I coughed out a laugh. "Not usually the word people use to describe him." He would be insulted, as he was a lethal arms expert, a professional sniper, a man with military training and expertise who was tapped to do the gravest of missions. "You will see him again later, I'm sure." I wasn't jealous that she wanted to see him. Not that I would ever admit aloud anyway.

I offered Erin my elbow, and she took it. "Please, let Oscar take your bags," I told her, and she tipped her chin up to look at me. "And I'll escort you to your suite."

She rolled her eyes at me. "Okay." She handed over the pink luggage and matching bag, and I gripped her hand and walked her up the steps.

"Thank you."

Her gasp was audible as we reached the front door and Joseph, the man whose sole responsibility was to man the door, opened it to let us in.

She walked in beside me and looked up at the ceiling, down at the floor, at the Renoir on the wall, the Degas, the marble foyer, the Ming vase. I was more impressed by the Springsteen autograph I'd gotten at a concert when I was nineteen, but chances were, she wouldn't see that since it was framed in my bedroom. "Wow, Henryk! This place is insane!"

I nodded at Joseph as we made our way inside. "Yes, I suppose it is." It was, indeed, grand. I didn't notice it anymore, but to someone who didn't see it every day of their childhood, it probably was a display of ridiculousness.

Raymond strode into the foyer, and said, "Erin, I'll take you to the guest wing."

Erin tugged her hand out of the crook of my elbow as quickly as if she'd been caught touching me in a less appropriate spot. Her skin flushed. She cleared her throat. "I think Henryk was going to take me."

"I have a few things to sort out before tomorrow," I told her, then watched as Raymond walked beside her up the steps to the first landing where they would turn right toward the guest wing.

Francis walked to stand beside me, also watching her go. "I was not expecting you home so early."

Of course, he wasn't. I'd told him it would be much later based on my expectation that mother nature would do her job and thus the airline would be able to do its job and I would be signing papers now, then delivering my guests to the hotels of their choice.

"Change of plans." He'd dealt with the airline many a time in the past and he'd arranged these tickets. "Silas and Viktor's flight was delayed until tomorrow, so I brought Erin back here for tonight. The other two can meet us here tomorrow to sign the papers, then it's business as usual." Which included marrying someone else. I rolled my eyes. This was ridiculous, but duty was birth right and the arranged marriage was my duty. It was a match beneficial to my country. Advantage. But to me, it felt as if I'd been sold to the highest bidder.

Francis frowned at me, and I knew what was coming. I'd heard it all before. It was why we'd decided to do it this way. "I'm not sure that's the right choice, Your Highness. Once they find out who you are, there will be a demand for money for their signatures, and that's assuming they sign at all and don't attempt to extort you." This was a man who was probably tired of this particular sermon. I'd heard it about ten times in the last two days. "Being married to you would be quite lucrative for them."

My head ached behind my eyes, and I pinched the bridge of my nose. I didn't know if there was correlation or if it helped—I don't think it did—but it bought me a second. "I know, Francis. But the war cabinet meeting is in the morning, and I must attend."

"I could have found accommodations for Miss Wright in the city," Francis argued, stepping dangerously close to the invisible line we maintained as employer/employee, even when we were friendly. "I still can."

I stared at him silently until he took a step back. "Yes, sir. Will you and Miss Wright be having dinner in the great hall?"

I glanced at my watch. Seven p.m. already. "Yes. Thank you, Francis."

My steward bowed his head and walked off in the direction of the kitchen.

I retired to the study to unpack everything I'd taken to the city apartment and to take a minute to compose myself.

I wanted her, the American girl who'd grown into an American woman. Desire burned through me to kiss her until she moaned my name and fell into my bed. Being with her would be different from any experience I'd had before.

But it was impossible. I couldn't sleep with her then divorce her.

I went to my room, showered and changed from my suit into a pair of jeans and a sweater. It took a minute for my heart to stop thumping. I couldn't stop thinking of her. Couldn't stop my body from responding to the thought of feeling her skin against mine, her hands on me, her mouth.

How had I let this happen?

CHAPTER 5

Erin

I stood in the middle of a guest suite the size of my entire apartment and the one next to it. If I'd been capable, I would have done cartwheels because it was *that* big.

"This is amazing," I gushed, staring at the lush drapes that covered the floor-to-ceiling windows, the wooded bed frame carved with leaves and flowers, the jeweled chandelier hanging from the ceiling.

Ray shut the door and put my suitcases on the bed. "There's time for a shower before dinner if you want to freshen up."

"God, yes!" My excitement came in an unreasonable amount and I smiled softly, like a lady. "Thank you. That's a great idea." Same sentiment, less enthusiasm.

Ray walked over to a door at the other side of the room and pushed it open. "Private bathroom is through here."

Oh, I had to see what a bathroom in a royal castle looked like. The clawfoot tub was a swimming pool. White marble as far as the eye could see with gold faucets. Probably real gold. This room was also large enough to turn a few cartwheels, and I looked at Ray. "I might need a map to take a..." My mouth twisted. "Shower."

His eyebrows pushed together, and his lips thinned. "I don't understand. The shower is in the lavatory beside the..." He smiled. "Are you teasing me, Miss Wright?"

I chuckled. "Caught me."

"Yes, ma'am." He nodded. "If you don't need me anymore, I'll leave you to it." Ray nodded to the door, gave a slight bow in my direction then stood straight and tall.

He really did have the most incredible posture.

"Thanks for all your help today, Ray," I said, and laid my sweater over the back of a chair, sighing into the silence. After being in an airport then a plane, then another airport and more travel, it was nice just to stand still in the quiet.

"You're welcome, Miss Erin." He winked at me, then left quietly.

I should've asked him about the backpacking trip, but I'd been too awed by the room, by the size of a bathtub. After I walked around the bedroom gaping at the furnishings, I found my way back to the huge bathroom where I took a long, hot shower and let all the tension of the last week just wash away.

When I walked back into the bedroom, I threw open my suitcase and stared at a whole lot of sweaters and jeans, shorts and tank tops. I had hiking clothes and Lichtenstein-in-the-city clothes, but I hadn't planned for dinner in a castle.

What was I supposed to wear?

I rummaged through the first suitcase, then the second, smaller bag. "Ah-ha!" Thank God I'd thrown in a black dress at the last minute. It was cotton, and it was more suited for a casual lunch in the sun than a grand ballroom, but it was as close I had to appropriate for this situation.

I dragged on some nice underwear so at least I'd feel good underneath the basic black, then pulled on the dress and stared at myself in the mirror.

Oh, yeah, that's way too much cleavage.

I grabbed a pink button-up jacket and finished the look with some black, flat sandals.

A bit of makeup and a brush through my hair and I was as ready to go as I would ever be.

I grabbed my cell phone, took a quick pic and shot it to Bree.

Proof of life.

She didn't respond right away, but with the time difference, I guessed she was still probably at work.

I opened the door and stared up and down the long, carpeted expanse. Which direction was the dining room? At first, I didn't see a single person. Should I just start walking and hope for the best?

Then a woman in a maid's outfit hurried down the hall. She was about my age, but her brisk pace and surly expression didn't exactly make her seem accessible.

"Hello," I said. But she didn't even look at me. Instead, she pointed her gaze straight ahead and continued so that I had no choice but to follow her. "Hello?" I called out again. "Can you help me, please?"

She stopped and turned toward me then bobbed a curtsey like I was some sort of royalty. "Of course, ma'am." And now I had her rapt attention.

"Great," I said, waiting for her to lift her gaze to meet mine. "I think I'm supposed to be meeting Henryk for dinner. Could you tell me how to get there?" I liked that she didn't look at me like I was pathetic for asking. This place was huge, and I was a directional dolt. Combined, this was my nightmare.

The maid ducked her head. "Of course, ma'am. Follow me."

The castle was so impressive, I kept stopping to stare at paintings and pieces of furniture along the way It was like a Hollywood movie set, ornate and intricate, but without the tell-tale cracks in the façade. The whole place was like nothing I'd ever seen before in real life.

By the time I was finally shown into a huge room containing a long dining table, the maid's sighing had taken an annoyed tone. She made a quick exit as soon as she delivered me to the door.

"Come in, please." Henryk walked over to meet me.

He looked even more scrumptious than he had earlier, in a casual gray shirt that was open at the neck and a pair of black jeans.

His eyes lit up as he stared at me, his gaze raking my body and settling a little too long on my cleavage, not that I minded.

"You look lovely."

I took his hand with a smile and my skin flushed. His hand was warm, his touch gentle as he led me to the table. "I wasn't sure what was appropriate to wear to eat in a castle. Sorry."

"Don't be sorry. You look perfect."

We sat together at one end, where only two places had been set. Even though I was quite happy with the thought of it just being us, I looked at him and the thoughts in my head were spinning dangerously. Us. Together. On the table.

I swallowed hard. "It's just us?" I asked Not that I wanted anyone else to join us. My thoughts were leading me in directions they shouldn't, and more people here at the table likely wouldn't have stymied the effect. But I was glad it was just the two of us.

Henryk nodded. "Yes. My parents are in London."

"You still live with your parents?" That was a surprise. I'd loved my parents immensely but living with them was unthinkable. My mother woke every morning at dawn's early light and thought because she was up, everyone in the house should also be awake. And there were only so many baseball games a girl could watch and care about batting averages or ERAs. A grin spread across my face.

There was nothing wrong with living with his parents, of course. I wasn't one to judge. And the "house" was big enough that chances were, if they didn't want to, they wouldn't have had to see each other.

Henryk tilted his head and stared as if he was trying to figure out why I would ask such a question. "Yes, I do." Maybe it was odd to him that I didn't live with mine. I didn't ask.

I hadn't lived with my folks since I turned eighteen and went off to college.

I glanced at the place setting. There was a lot of silverware for one person and one meal. "So, what's for dinner?"

There were a few men in matching whites standing against the walls, but other than that, there wasn't another soul to be seen. And certainly, no food.

Henryk smiled and lifted his hand. "We shall see, though I assume Cook will have made something traditional. She usually does."

A line of servants walked into the room then, each carrying a covered tray. My eyes went wide. That was a lot of food and we were only two people. One of the staff put a tray in front of me and another set a tray in front of Henryk then they removed the silver covers by the round handles on top.

The scent of smoked pork wafted on the air and my mouth watered.

"This is *Judd mat Gaardebounen*," Henryk explained. "Smoked pork, broad beans and boiled potatoes."

"Smells delicious." And the presentation was artful, aesthetically pleasing in a way I'd never noticed food to be. I was almost ashamed to cut into it with my fork, but I was also hungry and hunger won. I took a bite and salty goodness burst over my tongue. Oh God. This was so good. "Mmm. Yum."

"Would you like some wine?" He waved to one of the servers, who moved forward with a bottle of what looked to be pinot noir. Henryk nodded and sat silently as the waiter poured us each a glass.

I didn't usually drink much, but when in Rome... "Thank you."

As we finished each course, a new one was set in front of us and I ate. And ate. And ate. Each plate was more delicious than the last. When we were finally at dessert, I sat back in my chair. It was a fluffy pudding kind of thing—coconut, if I had to guess by the scent—with whipped cream and toasted coconut on top.

When I sat back again, I'd never been so full. "That was incredible. Thank you."

Henryk cocked his head and even with narrow eyes as if he couldn't believe what he was seeing, he was gorgeous enough that looking at him after a few seconds of not looking at him made my breath catch. "It's nice to see a woman who enjoys her food."

I frowned. "Who wouldn't enjoy a meal like that?"

He leaned back in his chair and studied me. It took him a few long seconds to reply. "You'd be surprised."

I leaned back, mirroring his pose and sighed. "So, tell me about yourself, Henryk. What do you do now?" This was a royal castle and he was sitting in a formal dining room, being served. "Do you work? Or is managing this castle a job unto itself? This place is huge." If he didn't manage this castle, that meant something wholly different. I didn't want to think about it. That would make me reconsider every second and every word I'd said since I got here and I didn't need that kind of pressure right now.

Henryk chuckled. "It is pretty big, I will grant you that, Erin." He steepled his fingers in front of his mouth, but I could still see the faint smile behind those fingers. "I guess you could say I work for the country and my family. Not in a modern sense, more in a traditional sense." Rather than hyperventilate as I digested what he hadn't said, I nodded and pretended he'd said he was the janitor.

"Yes, I'm getting that *traditional* vibe." I smiled and nodded. I loved hearing him talk, but he wasn't overly forthcoming. And a girl had to do what a girl had to do. "So, tell me about this woman you're arranged to marry." In some cultures, arranged marriage was a thing. But Lichtenstein seemed as socially forward as South Carolina. I had a lot of questions but I wondered what kind of woman agreed to this kind of thing. I also wanted to know how the arrangement had come about. Who decided this kind of thing?

Henryk shook his head and he looked down at his hands in his lap. "She's from a neighboring family."

Somehow, I doubted he meant his next-door neighbor. Hell,

from my room in the castle, I could see far and wide and there hadn't been any structure close. "You're marrying your next-door *neighbor*?" It just didn't fit. Nor did I understand. And I wanted more information. "Is she nice? Do you *want* to marry her?"

He blinked like I'd asked if she had an extra eyeball or a third arm. "Pardon me?"

"I know. Americans, right? I'm curious though." I swirled my finger around a design in the tablecloth. Maybe it was rude to ask, but I didn't care. "I mean, before I divorce you so you can marry another woman, I want to make sure you're happy." This time I smiled.

He didn't return the gesture but continued studying his hands. "I don't know her that well."

"Is she beautiful?" I couldn't imagine him with anyone less than a beauty. I didn't honestly want to imagine him with anyone else.

He nodded. "She's beautiful." Of course, she was. "She's no you."

My skin flushed with heat. "Do you love her?" It was the second time I asked the question and the second time he didn't answer, so I expanded on the thought. "It's very strange to me. I can't imagine marrying someone I didn't love."

"You Americans and your *love*." He used air quotes. "I'm sure you know that America's divorce rate is over fifty percent?" He was mocking the idea of love.

"Coming from someone who's been bound in marriage since he was seven and now has to get divorced, you can imagine how ironic I find your disdain toward love."

"I didn't profess my undying love when we were seven either."

I laughed. That was true, he hadn't. "You were the one who

said you wanted to marry me." Whether he was or was not, he'd still said yes. Slipped my daisy ring on my finger and allowed me to put mine on him. I took a big sip from my wine glass and continued, "And if the grown-up version of you is saying we're screwed no matter what, so we may as well marry someone our parents choose for us, then I'm sad for you and I miss seven year old Henryk."

His jaw fell open then snapped shut.

I pressed my lips together, musing over the idea. I couldn't imagine the kind of guy my parents would choose for me. Probably a dairy farmer. Mom liked fresh milk. Or a cop. Dad liked honor and duty. To be honest, I didn't think my parents would choose anyone. They respected my choices and my ability to make a choice.

I closed my eyes and leaned my head back against the chair. The wine was kicking in. "My head is spinning, Henryk," I admitted.

His chair scraped against the floor, and I forced my eyes open. He stepped up next to me with a concerned look, and I stared at him. "I'll escort you to your room," he said softly and held out his hand. I aimed to slip mine into his, and I had to close one eye to hit the mark. "You haven't actually had that much to drink, but you're probably suffering from jetlag. And the wine on top of that..."

True. I yawned and shifted closer to him, suddenly exhausted. I couldn't remember how far it was to my room, but I wouldn't have minded a rolling chair or a scooter.

I clung to his arm as he walked me out of the dining room and down the hallway. A muscle in his arm flinched and I could feel the power in him. "Was I rude to you?"

He stopped walking and looked down at me. "When we were children?"

I laughed and it felt too loud and long, so I cut it off. "No, tonight. Was it rude to ask if you love your fiancé or if you want to marry her?" He was kind, helping me to my room, arranging for my accommodations tonight, feeding me.

He squeezed my arm gently. "No. But no one else has ever asked me that."

I leaned my head against his shoulder as we started walking again. "That makes me sad." And it did. I didn't want to think of him as stuck in a marriage with someone he didn't want to be married to.

He chuckled and slowed as we reached my bedroom door. "To answer your question a little more honestly, I'm not sure how I feel about marrying someone I've only met once or twice." He smiled when I tilted my chin up to look at him. "It's probably about the same as remaining married to someone I met when I was a child." It felt like we'd been walking for an hour. I wanted to sit, but I let him continue leading me down the hallway as he spoke. "I've known since I was young that my duty was to make an advantageous match." Whatever that meant.

I turned toward him and used my body to crowd him backward against the wall. I pressed closer and stared up at his big blue eyes. "You're the most beautiful man I've ever seen in real life." Sure, there were magazine guys and book cover guys, but those men had the benefit of photoshop and makeup. Henryk was the real deal. And I wanted to stare at him until every pore and bit of chin stubble was imprinted in my brain.

This time he smiled and his cheeks reddened. "Thank you."

"It's true." I gave him an up and down look that left no doubt.

"And you're built like you know your way around a weight bench." He chuckled and I couldn't move much closer without crawling into his clothes. But I sure as hell tried. I could feel all the valleys and planes of his body, the ridged, hard muscle. "You, my friend, could have any woman in the world." Not a wine-induced exaggeration, either. Although, wine might have had something to do with the ease of which I said the words.

"Any woman?" And then he shook his head. "I wish that were true." His smile was gentle as he took both my hands, lifted them to his lips and pressed kisses to the fingers of my left hand, and then my right. "Erin, it's you who deserves the world. I'm just sorry I can't be the one to give it to you." He pushed off the wall and smiled

I sighed. Men didn't say things like that. Not in my experience, anyway. I could've stood there listening to him say it for a good couple of hours. But instead, I laid my hand on his chest over his heart and absorbed the soft steady thud, imagining his beating in time with mine. "I suppose I should get to bed now. The jet lag —"To demonstrate, I yawned."—seems to be catching up."

This time, his smile was sad. "By tomorrow we won't be married any longer and you'll be free to roam all over Europe at your leisure."

I nodded even though the thought wasn't as pleasing as it was a few hours ago. "Yeah. Well, goodnight, Henryk."

He inclined his head in an old-fashioned manner. "Good night, Erin."

I grabbed hold of his hand and tugged him back. I had a belly full of alcohol courage and I wasn't afraid to use it. "I want to kiss you and I want you to kiss me." Oh, yeah. That was exactly what I wanted.

His eyes burned with desire. I wasn't the most experienced woman in the world, but I knew desire when I saw it, even though he said, "I shouldn't."

I lifted my chin, bringing our lips closer. "You should." My voice was a whisper, but it sounded loud inside my head. I wasn't quite begging yet, but I was on the verge.

When he moved in, slowly, deliberately, I sucked in a shallow breath and he cupped my face between his hands. "Erin." It wasn't more than my name, but it was the best sound I'd ever heard. He stared into my eyes and I never wanted to look away.

But then he lowered his head and his mouth brushed mine, slow and soft before he came back in and the heat of his lips branded mine. An ache started low in my belly as he continued this sensuous caress. The world floated away.

CHAPTER 6

Henryk

What started as a chaste kiss meant to satisfy my own curiosity quickly flared into need and desire and heat so potent I couldn't stop kissing her.

Her lips were soft, and she tasted like red wine and summer.

I pressed deeper, sliding my tongue between her lips. When she moaned, I swallowed the sound and slid my hands down her body, gripping her waist and pulling her more tightly against my body.

She wrapped her arms around my neck and pushed closer.

Oh, fuck. I'm in trouble.

My cock twitched with need and the urge was strong to pick Erin up and carry her into the private suite behind us. I wanted her. I wanted to feel her skin, the heat of her body, the gentle curves. I was so ready.

Tearing my lips from hers, I stepped back, panting with the effort it took to stop touching her. Stop *kissing* her.

I stared at her, enchanted by the beauty that was so intense I didn't have words to describe. Her cheeks were flushed with color and her lips bruised from my kisses. Somehow, though I didn't remember doing it, I'd mussed her long, dark hair.

I looked away. No way would I be able to walk away from her or cool my lust if I continued staring like a man dying to touch her. Instead, I thought of duty. Mine specifically. To my country, to my father, to the woman I was to marry. As much as I hated it, my duty was probably the only thing that would stop me from taking her to bed.

"I'll see you in the morning, Erin." My voice was a deep rasp, and I'd yet to catch my breath. I sound like an eighty-year-old who'd just run a marathon.

"Are you all right?" Her concern was enough to shame me, but I brushed my hand down her cheek then pulled away before the one last touch I allowed myself turned into more.

I met her gaze and she pulled her lower lip between her teeth. It was innocent, sweet almost, and it drove me wild. My heart rate kicked up and my stomach clenched. I groaned. "Erin, I want you almost more than I can control and if you continue to look at me with such... like that..."I pointed at her face, and she tilted her head and I was too close to losing my control. "I'm not going to be able to walk away from you. And for our mutual good, I must."

It could've been her beauty or the nostalgia of worshipping her back then, imagining her all these years and not even coming close to how incredible she was, or it could've been nothing more than the intensity of this moment, but I wanted her so badly I ached with need.

She slid her tongue along her lower lip in a quick swipe and I wanted to taste her again. "What if..."

I held up a hand and she stopped speaking, thank fuck. "Goodnight, Erin."

"Counteroffer?"

Pathetic as I was, she didn't need to say more. I quickly closed the distance between us and took her into my arms again.

Her arms wound around me and she clung. I was being held by a woman who wanted me as a man, not as a king. This one didn't know what I was or who I was to be. She knew Henryk, the man.

Henryk, King of Lichtenstein. Nothing mattered except that I was to be king. And she would be gone. I couldn't compromise either of us with an affair that could destroy us both. I had a duty to my kingdom.

I slowed the kiss and finally pulled back enough so I could rest my forehead against hers. "You are the most incredible woman."

She curled her fingers into the front of my shirt. "Then don't stop."

I sighed, heavy and long. "Because you're leaving tomorrow, and I don't want to do anything that we would regret tonight."

She pulled back like I'd burned her. "Oh my God. You're right. And you're engaged." She shook her head. "What was I thinking?" And then she turned, no longer talking to me, but still talking. "What the hell? He's engaged to someone else. *Belongs* to someone else."

She staggered to her door grabbed hold of the handle, pushed it down and disappeared inside.

"Erin!" I called out because I was pathetic and I couldn't stop myself. I needed to see her face for one more second.

"Yes?" She turned back to face me, biting her lip again and tempting me to indulge.

"Thank you for coming. You have no idea how much it means to my country."

She shrugged like it didn't matter, but the weight of this moment sat on my shoulders like a boulder even when she smiled. "It's okay."

It wasn't okay. It was extraordinary. It was beyond what was required. It was... "Just the same, I want you to know I'll forever remain in your debt as will Lichtenstein."

She smiled this time, though it was a little wobbly. "Good night, Henryk."

"Good night."

She closed the door, and I turned and stomped down the hallway.

Fucking responsibilities.

I growled on the way to my bedroom, slammed the door, and sat on the edge of the bed. I'd never met a woman like Erin. She was charming and beautiful. I was enchanted. And the kisses were... bliss. Heaven. More than I deserved.

My cock was still hard and it wouldn't take much to finish off, but instead, I went to the ensuite to freeze myself in a frigid shower that didn't cool my burning thoughts of sliding inside of her.

When I finally crawled into bed, loneliness swept over me. Normally, I didn't mind being alone, but being with Erin highlighted exactly how alone I was. Mine was a solitary role, until I was married, at least. Rather, married again.

I hadn't wanted to admit it to Erin, but one of the main reasons I'd agreed to my arranged marriage was so I could start a family, have a wife and children.

I was tired of being alone. Tired of all the articles questioning my bachelorhood, my sexuality, the women I "squired" around the country. I'd contacted the tabloids more than once to protest the word squire but it never worked. A marriage would stop all that. I hoped so, anyway.

And while we were of the same status and the same lifestyle, there were no guarantees that she and I would get along. I worried every night that I was going to end up in a Prince Charles/Princess Di situation and the world had already endured that once. No monarchy would survive it again.

I sighed and tried for sleep. Worrying would do me no good now. Only time would tell if marrying the woman my parents had chosen for me would be a good idea or a disaster.

I woke at five-thirty a.m. and started my day as usual with an hour in my personal gym, a quick shower, a spot check of my notes for the upcoming cabinet meeting, and then a brisk walk to the dining room by seven.

"Good morning." Erin was already seated at the table, her head in her hands.

She looked up as I approached, her skin ashen. "I find absolutely nothing good about it."

I laughed as Jordy poured me a cup of coffee. "Perhaps too much wine last night?" I nodded to Jordy who moved to her side of the table and poured. "The coffee should help. How do you take it?"

She nodded, then held the sides of her head again. "Cream and sugar."

Jordy reached for the small serving pitcher of creamer, but I shook my head and he smiled and backed away. I was happy to serve Erin. "Here you go."

I sat at the head of the table and reached for a slice of fruit. "You should try a piece of toast. It will settle your stomach." In my younger days, when I was busy trying to figure a way around giving myself to my country, I'd had no choice but to learn a thing or two about hangovers and how to rid myself of them.

"Please don't mention food." Erin shook her head and wrapped both hands around her cup of coffee. "I didn't think I drank that much last night."

"The jetlag amplifies the effects," I told her, also acquainted with travel while drinking. "Eat. And drink plenty of water. The only other cure is time."

She sighed and glanced up at me. "I'm sorry about last night." Her voice was soft, but she met my gaze and held it. The sincerity was appreciated but hardly necessary.

I took a scoop of eggs and a piece of toast. "What for?"

"For throwing myself at you." She shook her head, then widened her eyes "I don't usually... ever...I'm sorry."

"Yes, you mentioned." Heat surged through me. "I need to apologize too." When I looked at her, the words tumbled out. "I wanted to stay with you. I'm sorry I walked away." I swallowed, gulped, and the words were out there. I couldn't take them back.

"Oh, shit."

"Excuse me?" That certainly wasn't the reaction I'd been hoping for.

"I mean... I didn't... I wanted you to say... that." Her words were broken by breaths and then she blinked up at me, eyes wider. "Really?"

I nodded because it was going to take a second to find words.

When I finally did, all I managed was, "Yes." And then I smiled. "You're beautiful, Erin."

Pink inched up from her throat to her cheeks. "Thank you."

I leaned forward and lowered my voice because some things the staff here didn't need to know. "I've never wanted anyone the way I wanted you." Truth be told, I still wanted her. The last few hours apart when sleep should've deadened the need had done nothing to make me want her less. "But, Erin, if anything were ever to happen between us, I'd need us to both be sober and willing."

She nodded and reached for a piece of toast. "Sober, it is."

I ate slowly, wishing and hoping, wondering and considering, but it could never happen for us. My life was an obstacle. My status. The fact I was promised to someone else.

Francis walked into the dining room, clipboard in hand. It was time to start my official day and that always began with the official briefing of my schedule. "Your... Henryk." He coughed loudly to cover his slip.

I wanted to laugh at him but it had been Francis' idea to pretend I wasn't royalty, which meant everyone had to refer to me by my first name. Protocol suffered, but for the sake of national security, it could be ignored.

"Good morning, Francis." Protocol be damned but there was no reason to be less than courteous.

"Good morning." He tilted his head and bowed in my direction. "Your meeting starts in fifteen minutes."

I stood and buttoned my jacket. "Thank you, Francis. I'll leave now. Have Davis bring the car around." He was my morning driver. "Will you be available to help Erin this morning?"

Francis nodded, his lips twisted with annoyance. His job as my assistant was to deal with whatever situation arose or whatever detail I needed handled. Erin was such a detail, even though Francis generally found the female situations distasteful. But he would do what I asked simply because I asked it.

"Yes," he said, his tone clipped. "I will stay with her and arrange travel plans while we wait for the arrival of the other two Americans."

Erin stood. "Oh, that's right! Viktor and Silas arrive today, don't they?" I hadn't seen them since that day in the park, but I didn't know if Erin had or not. "Can I ride to the airport to pick them up?"

A jolt of jealousy shot through me, unexpected, and annoying. I looked at Francis. I didn't even know what time the flight was to arrive.

"Raymond has already departed to pick them up," Francis said calmly, but he was lying and I wondered why. "We can arrange for your continued travel while you wait for them to arrive." Francis didn't leave room for negotiation.

Erin nodded and sat down again.

"I'll return in a few hours," I informed. "We can sign the papers then and you can all be on your way." It sounded brusque, but I was smarting with jealousy. I walked away though I would rather have stayed with her.

The amount of effort it took to leave her surprised me. I stopped at the bottom of the steps before I climbed into the car. Then, at the edge of the drive, I asked Davis to wait a moment. When I couldn't justify going back for her, I had him drive on. Duty called, as it always did. And I was nothing if not dutiful.

* * *

Erin

As I watched Henryk walk away, a cold sadness seeped into my soul. When he left, it was like he took the warmth with him. I couldn't explain it clearly. I doubt if it was able to be explained. I'd only known him—not counting a day when I was a child—one day. Less, actually. But I was affected, and it was his fault.

I shivered and pulled my sweater tighter around me as we walked into what could only have been Francis's office. It was elegant with a chandelier in the center of the room, a desk that was a thousand years old if it was a day but still gleamed like it had only just been polished. His chair was one of those fancy modern ones with lumbar support and crazy gold armrests. Nearer to the door was a sofa flanked on each end by chairs that faced one another while the sofa faced a fireplace.

"Would you like a fire?" He nodded to the stone hearth.

I shivered again. "Yes, please."

He snapped his fingers and a manservant moved forward.

"Oh, I didn't mean to create more work for anyone."

Francis sat down in the chair opposite me and pulled a pen from his inner breast pocket. He smiled, poised to write on a pad of paper beside his computer keyboard. "Not at all. Now, let's talk about your planned travels while in Europe."

I nodded and took another sip of coffee, not asking for the Advil I so desperately needed for my pounding head. "Okay." I wasn't sure if I liked Francis. He was a little pompous for my taste, and wore a faint sneer on his face every time he looked at me. I was glad I didn't have to work with him long-term. He was one of those people who seemed to suck the joy out of living. All I could think was, *poor Henryk.*

But he was obviously here to help me now, so I smiled at him and tried to ignore his attitude. "Thank you for assisting me, Francis."

"Quite. So, you mentioned Spain, and I took the liberty of researching some accommodations for you." He opened his padfolio and began pulling out pamphlets.

I took one, my jaw dropping. "This isn't the sort of place I planned to stay." Five-star accommodations with gourmet dining. First, I couldn't afford that kind of place, and even if Henryk was footing the bill, I couldn't ask that.

Francis's brow furrowed. "Is there a problem?"

Uh-oh. His sneer had shifted to a scowl. Now, I'd offended him. I stared at the photo of the suite that had private butler service and twenty-four-hour room service, plus its own private beach. "I was going to backpack. Something like *this* isn't in my budget." I showed him the suite and shook my head.

I had some spending money, but if I worked ten hours a day at my crappy job every day for the rest of my life, there was no way I'd be able to afford even a single night at a place like this.

Francis waved a dismissive hand. "Henryk is not worried about the cost. He's promised a vacation for your trouble." He looked up and smiled but it was one of those that said he was trying to be patient and it wasn't going well.

It didn't matter to me what Henryk had promised, I couldn't let him pay for a place like this one. "I don't need anything nearly so extravagant."

"How long are you staying?" I might actually have no say in the matter.

"I planned for two weeks."

His smile was softer now and if I lived to be a hundred and some genius woman came out with a guidebook for maneuvering around them, I was never going to understand men. "Well, let's book you two weeks' accommodations, and if you need to extend your time, we can do that."

"I really..." I shook my head. This was opulent and extravagant and what did it say about me if I let Henryk pay for a place like this. I probably wouldn't be comfortable in a place like that. Not only that, but I wouldn't look the part. Wouldn't fit it. "I should..."

"Miss Wright, you're doing Lichtenstein a considerable kindness and Henryk would like to repay your courtesy." He cocked an eyebrow and I sighed. When I didn't answer, his stern expression softened. "All right, then. Spain is the first stop. And where would you like to go next? France? England? The Maldives?"

I shrugged. "I've never traveled outside of the United States before. I don't want to waste time backtracking." I chewed my lips. Hated to ask, but I only had a couple weeks, so I wanted to get the most out of the experience as I could. "Could you suggest an itinerary?"

Francis tilted his head and smiled. "Of course."

I sat back and let the expert guide me. After all, this whole experience had started off like something straight out of a dream, so I was going to roll with it and go where this wild ride led me.

CHAPTER 7

Erin

I let Francis talk me into spending a week in Spain, a week in France, and then a week in London. I'd need to email my boss and ask for the additional time off, but since this morning when all my travel wishes became travel realities, I couldn't imagine going back to my old life. Not yet, at least. I had some living to do.

I wanted to be inspired by my life. And thus far, the most exciting thing that had ever happened to me was finding out that my pretend wedding during a second-grade trip to DC was a real deal marriage, so I would've been a fool to pass up this trip. Certainly not to rush back to a dead-end job where I could've been replaced in the space of ten minutes and a promotion of the coffee girl.

How I would ever be able to pay my rent if my boss fired me, I had no idea, but that was a problem for another day. Right now, I was on vacation and I was determined to enjoy myself.

When Francis finished organizing my travel, I excused myself because I was hung over and wanted a shower. I let the spray of steaming hot water wash away my headache and then I used some scented shampoo from an electric dispenser and then conditioned. I even did my makeup. The guys would be here soon, and I wanted to look my best. They were my husbands, after all. For a few more hours, anyway. I needed to look good.

I dressed in my favorite jeans and a tank, a long-sleeve top and my new black sweater. Despite the fires burning in most rooms, it was still colder than I was used to over here, so I dressed accordingly.

After a quick check in the mirror, a fluff of my curls, and a slow, deep breath, I wandered back to the foyer. My stomach twisted with nerves, and I was one flutter away from taking flight. I just couldn't control my excitement.

I paced the foyer, checking the time on my phone every few minutes. Likely I looked anxious, but was unable to stop. I couldn't wait for Ray to get back with Silas and Viktor.

"Can I get something for you, miss?" a maid asked as she approached with an empty tray.

I shook my head. "No. I'm fine, thank you. I—"

The front doors suddenly opened and Ray walked in, dressed in black jeans and a blue shirt. The outfit made him simultaneously gorgeous and lethal looking. How had I not noticed that yesterday? He moved quietly, graceful and lithe, a man who could slip in and out of shadows if necessary. I stared for a second.

Was he Henryk's personal assistant or something more sinister? Maybe Henryk's money came from the proceeds of crime? My imagination took off, and I shook my head to dispel the silly thoughts. Henryk was just a businessman. Obviously, a very one successful enough to buy a royal castle , but still...

"Hello, Miss Wright," Ray said as he approached, scanning my casual outfit with an appreciative eye. He curled his finger under my chin and used it to lift my head. "You're looking well today."

"Thank you." I grinned at him, at ease with Ray despite the fact I'd known him less than a day. "Did you pick up Silas and Viktor?"

He nodded. "Yes." Then he leaned in and his breath was warm against my cheek. "Two more husbands coming your way."

Heat flooded my face. It sounded so ridiculous, even now. *Husbands.*

I turned to the front doors and two guys walked in, wrapped in huge, puffy winter jackets.

"Fuck, it's freezing," the blond said as he stepped in the door. He was tall with the body of an athlete—slender and wiry. His hair was pushed back in one of those artful styles that required gel and mousse and clay. But it was his eyes—gray blue—that drew me in. I assumed, since he was blond when we were young, that this one was Silas.

The other one had shorter, dark hair and a neck tattoo creeping up behind his ear.

The blond pushed shut the door again, then they both peeled off their jackets. It was an *oh my* moment and it took a second for my brain to resume normal function. Wow.

"Erin?" Silas asked, his gaze sweeping the length of my body. I stood still and waited until he was finished.

I stared back at him. "Silas?" I whispered, looking beyond the blond hair for any other signs of the stout little boy I'd once known.

"Yeah." He moved in as if he was going to hug me and then I made it awkward by shifting my arms so that we would bump into one another arm first. He moved his, I moved mine. We were doing the reverse robot until he finally got close enough to wrap his arms around me and we both laughed.

Just that easily, my shy awkwardness dissipated. He set me on my feet again, as Viktor watched us from the side. I turned to him and grinned. "Hi, Viktor."

"Erin." He exuded cool guy calm. Even his smile was slightly subdued as if he were too cool to be excited. "It's been a long time."

"It has!" I exclaimed, taking in all the little details. Viktor's gray sweater that matched Silas's eyes. And Silas was an inch or so taller than Viktor. Viktor had eyes that were so brown I almost couldn't tell where the pupil began. His legs were long, and his jeans fit him like they were tailor made. And Silas wore a blue sweater that made his eyes all the stormier. This was a moment I wanted etched into my memory. I was going to want to dissect it all later.

There wasn't much to indicate that these were the little boys who'd each slipped a daisy ring on my fingers.

"Wow. You guys... grew up." An understatement. They hadn't just grown up, they were hot.

We were all glancing from one to another. I didn't know if they'd kept in touch over the years or not and I wondered, but Viktor's gaze sharpened as he glanced at me and he smiled. My stomach fluttered. When Silas looked at me in the same way, the flutter got stronger.

"Yeah, well a lot changes in twenty years," Viktor said. One thing that didn't change was his smile. It was boyish and sweet, and I might've fallen a little bit in love standing in Henryk's foyer staring at him.

"It certainly does." If I sounded breathless, it was because I was.

Ray held his arm out to me. "I'm sure the three of you are hungry, and of course, you have a lot to catch up on."

I took Ray's arm since he was offering. "Where are we going?"

"To the northern sitting room. Lunch is being served there."

I was less queasy than I'd been earlier, but the thought of food made me waver. "Will Henryk be meeting us there?" I walked arm in arm with Ray out of the foyer and along one of the many grand hallways.

"Yes. He'll be there when his current meeting ends." He smiled down at me and there was a twinkle.

Ray showed us into a huge room with yet another a roaring fire, where a table against the wall was spread with a line of plattered food. Sandwiches and salads, hot food, cold food, fruit, charcuterie, cheeses, so many choices.

"I'm starving," Silas said, rubbing his hands together as he walked around me straight to the table.

"Thanks, Ray." It wasn't that I needed led into the room, but there wasn't a much better way to walk around the castle—the castle—than on this guy's arm.

He winked at me, then I watched his broad shoulders as he walked out the room.

I sat down in one of the dining chairs and reached for a bread roll. "The food here is delicious."

The table was set like a buffet and another long table with three place setting was beside it but closer to the center of the room. I sat at one side of the table and Silas took the spot beside me. When he set his plate down, he lifted the bottle of wine from where it sat between us and Viktor, and read the label. "This is a thousand-dollar bottle of Pinot Noir."

"Wine?" Silas asked, offering me the bottle.

I shook my head and held up my hand, stomach lurching. "God, no. I'm still hung over from last night."

He laughed. "When I'm hung over, I look like I've been hit by a bus." The look he gave me was heated and I sucked in a breath. "You do not look hung over." He glanced away from me and added a slice of roast beef to his plate. Softer, he said, "You're beautiful."

The temperature in here must've climbed like fifty degrees. I was warm from cheek to toe. And the way he was staring at me now didn't help. "Thank you." But I needed to change the subject. Fast. "You guys both look great. I don't know what I expected, but this is better."

"Better? What did you expect?" Viktor chuckled. "I, for one, expected you to be beautiful." He grinned. "And you are."

If I was keeping score, and I should've been, that was two *beautifuls* in about forty-five seconds.

There was a lot of testosterone in this room, a lot of muscle and so much handsome, my thoughts had no defense. I swallowed my suddenly lust-filled thoughts and tried to act as cool and collected as the men. "So, what do you two do?" I asked, glancing from one to the other.

Silas reached for the mashed potatoes. "We're in construction."

"Really? Together?" I smiled at him.

Viktor nodded and poured himself a glass of wine. "Yeah. We work together. We actually just started our own construction company."

Quite the husbands I had here. "That's awesome." I wasn't sure they knew each other when we originally met.

Silas nodded at me as he took a sip from his glass then smiled. "When we got the call from Francis, we'd just come from a meeting with a buyer of a house we flipped."

I'd been about to express my awe or some other ridiculous emotion when Viktor saved me. "Speaking of which," he said with a cheeky grin. "I did a little research before we left for Lichtenstein. Do you know who Henryk is?"

"*Who* he is?" I shrugged. "He's one of the little boys I married when I was seven." Although just by his smile, I knew that wasn't what he meant.

"I mean... do you know who he is?" Viktor repeated the question without any emphasis and I couldn't tell what message he was trying to convey.

"She doesn't know," Silas said, his grin as knowing as Viktor's, and I wasn't sure I liked being the only one who didn't know what was apparently a big secret. "Just tell her."

"Yeah, just tell me." I wasn't annoyed as much as I just felt out of the loop, like I was behind.

Viktor and Silas looked at each other, then stared at me as Viktor spoke. "He's the crown prince of Liechtenstein. The next king."

"He's what now?" Crown prince? Next king?

. . .

"What?" I knew what all of those words meant singularly, and I knew what they all meant as a team, but I didn't understand their correlation to Henryk.

"I told you she didn't know," Silas said, nodding at Viktor like he had indeed said I didn't know. I had too much information to unpack to worry about the fact they seemed to be enjoying too much that I hadn't known.

"How could you not know?" Viktor demanded. "Look where you are, Erin. The wealth. The royal castle. The servants."

And now I felt stupid. How had I not known? "I thought..." I snapped my mouth shut. I'd been busy imagining a billionaire crime lord. Prince hadn't even been a thought.

A door closed behind us, and Silas and I twisted to look at Henryk striding into the room with a leather briefcase in hand.

"You're a prince? *The* prince?" I stared at him through narrowed eyes. Even though he'd never confirmed or denied anything—I hadn't asked—I felt lied to.

"I apologize for not telling you myself, Erin." He shot a pointed look at Viktor. "But my parents and my steward assumed you wouldn't sign the divorce papers if you knew who I was."

His *steward*? Oh. Francis.

Henryk reached the table and nodded at the guys. "Viktor. Silas. Thank you for coming all this way." He was about as warm as an icicle.

While they did a group round of handshakes, I sat digesting this revelation. Jet lag, hangovers, and big shocking news were not happy bedfellows.

Henryk is a prince. The next king.

I stared at him. "You were just an ordinary kid in that playground all those years ago."

He smiled down at me but there was a coldness in his eyes now that hadn't been there earlier. And while I couldn't blame him because he didn't really know me, he hadn't kissed me like he didn't trust me.

Annoyance bit into my shock, and I tightened my lips as Henryk said, "My parents are the king and queen. It wasn't a choice. And I was a *prince* back then, too. but on the playground I was Henryk."

Viktor glanced at me then at Henryk. "Your place is incredible."

"Thank you." Henryk didn't sit down. "If you would all join me in the office, we can get this paperwork signed and you can all be on your way." And the hospitable man of yesterday was gone. I didn't particularly care for his replacement.

"Why don't you sit down and we can all have a drink first?" Silas looked at me like I was going to jump onto the let's all have a drink bandwagon. I wasn't. "We haven't seen you in twenty years."

Henryk glanced from one of us to the other. "I'd rather just get the paperwork organized."

Viktor glanced at me and I shrugged. What else was I going to do?

"All right, then. Let's go get divorced." Viktor stood and held out his hand to me.

I glanced at Silas, then at Henryk. "Okay. Let's do it."

The shock was slowly wearing off and I realized the warm, sexy man I'd kissed last night had left the building. Yesterday, he was the grown-up version of the boy I'd played with as a child. Today, Henryk was a prince, official and distant. For me, it was time to stop daydreaming and move on. This wasn't a Cinderella story and I wasn't cut out for the part.

My legs wobbled when I stood, and I gratefully took Viktor's hand and smiled up at him. "Thank you."

Henryk walked across the room, and we followed.

"I can't believe this," I whispered to Viktor.

"Which part?"

The giggles took over. I stopped walking and laughed. Big belly laughs and they all stopped to stare at me.

"Erin?" Henryk cocked his head at me.

I pointed from me to Silas to Viktor. "We're married to a prince. All of us." I struggled to catch my breath and pull it together. Just when I thought I had it, I lost it again. "This is just insane."

And like I hadn't said quite enough yet, I added, "I'm a princess." And the giggles wouldn't end. "So are you and you." I pointed to Silas and Viktor.

"You weren't a princess. And you're entitled to nothing." *This* was the reason Henryk had hidden who he really was. He didn't trust any of us. If either of the boys, or me for that matter, refused to sign the paperwork then he was stuck, married to three people he didn't want to be married to.

"It isn't like I'm going to extort you for your freedom." For fuck's sake. But on the other hand, he didn't know me. The children we'd been then weren't the adults we were now. He certainly hadn't shown a single sign of having a stick shoved up his ass back then.

Viktor winked at me and I narrowed my eyes at him, but he was looking ahead at our prince "husband."

"My office is through here," Henryk said, inviting us into an office that was five times the size of the office Francis used. This one had floor to ceiling bookshelves that were full of books and had one of those rolling ladders in front. His desk was old and heavy, ornate with a shine to the wood that only came with love and care.

The warmth matched the man I'd had dinner with last night, but it certainly didn't match the prince standing in front of me now.

Henryk's tone was icy. "Shall we get to signing and then you can all get on with your lives." He really wanted us gone.

"And you can get on with yours." Silas sniped at a prince. We were American. Royalty wasn't our thing. "Itching to marry your stranger, are you?"

He almost smiled and I almost mentioned it, but I kept my lips clamped shut. How he'd gone from being so sweet to so snide, I couldn't understand. It was like he had a personality switch. "Yes, well..." Henryk opened his briefcase and took out bundles of papers.

I picked up a dip pen—who used these anymore—dipped it into the well of ink in front and poised it as if I was about to write on the mahogany desk. "Let's get on with it."

Henryk pointed at the contracts. "I've made five copies. One each for us, and one for filing with the authorities."

I glanced up at him, meeting his dark gaze and feeling a pang of regret. "Wouldn't want to hold up your wedding." I was bitter and didn't understand it. We didn't know each other beoynd what his body felt like under my palm, how his lips tasted, how his eyes darkened when with desire. But I hadn't even known he was a prince. This was for the best. Henryk stared at me, then nodded once. "Of course. It has to be this way."

I sighed and put the pen to paper. "All right. As you wish, *your highness.*"

Then it would be on to Spain, leaving my prince—indeed, leaving all three of my husbands—behind forever.

CHAPTER 8

Viktor

Erin signed all five copies of our weird-ass childhood marriage divorce papers, then handed the pen to Henryk. For being a prince, this guy was pretty normal looking. In fact, other than the custom-tailored suit that probably cost more than the house Si and I had just sold, he looked like any other guy. I didn't see any sign of a crown. Kind of disappointing, if I was honest.

He signed all five copies, then handed the pen to Silas. Si, business partner and best friend, looked at me, then shrugged and bent his head to chicken scratch his name across each of the contracts too.

When it came time for my turn, my gut told me not to do it. I wasn't sure why I had such a strong urge *not* to sign, but I usually followed my gut. It had taken me far over the years. So, when I took the pen from Silas's hand, I gripped it and stared at the three people I was allegedly married to. "I'm not sure about this."

Henryk groaned. "I knew it. One of you…" He shook his head.

Erin huffed, but I didn't know who she was huffing at. Maybe she wanted this too.

Silas simply shook his head. I put up my hands. "Hey, man. I don't want to be married to *you*. You're a guy. But Erin…" I met her gaze and smiled. "This feels like it's kind of meant to be. Maybe we shouldn't rush into breaking up."

Erin cocked an eyebrow. "We were seven." She shook her head. "And that doesn't feel like the kind of thing I should have to say." Her sigh was short but loud. "We were never together."

"But we could be," I said, and even I wasn't a hundred percent sure what I was thinking. "If we don't sign these forms, then maybe we could start something."

Erin's eyebrows rose high on her forehead. "The four of us?"

I glanced sideways at Henryk. "Well, not Mr. Fancy Pants over there, but the three of us. Why not?"

Silas and I didn't have a problem sharing a woman. We'd done it before.

Henryk crossed his arms and leaned back in his chair, nostrils flared, anger emanating off him. "If this is about money, I'm paying you to sign. What more do you want?"

I rolled my eyes, mimicking his pinched facial expression. "You can keep your fucking money. We aren't paupers who need you to finance us with your inherited wealth. We have a business *we* built." I was being an asshole and I didn't give a shit. He'd crossed a line. If we were after money, we would've demanded it a lot sooner.

Erin put her hand on my arm, and shivers coursed over my skin. "I'm going to Spain for a week, then France and England.

Francis has already organized it all. Do you and Silas want to come with me?" She looked up at me with her big, beautiful eyes and I was lost. She could've asked me to rob a bank and I would've been powerless to do more than agree.

How ironic would it be if I'd met my soul mate when I was seven years old? And now I was about to divorce her!

I forced myself to stay cool despite the heady effect of her touch. "Yeah, that would be great."

She tapped the desk. "Then sign these and we can move on to Spain. Together."

My gaze snapped up to the prince, who had made a strange type of pained noise. It was almost imperceptible, but I had excellent hearing. "What's your problem?"

Henryk shook his head. "Nothing at all. Please. Sign. And I'll be happy to organize European holidays for all three of you if that's what you wish."

My gut twisted again, my instincts screaming at me not to leave Mr. Fancy Pants behind. I growled, then bent my head to sign the first copy. Then the second. I glanced up again. Jesus. This guy wore his heart on his sleeve. Along with his anger and loneliness.

I threw down the pen. "Shit."

"What's wrong now?" Henryk demanded.

I scrubbed my fingers over my scalp. "You owe us for this, right?"

Henryk straightened so that he was now ramrod-stiff and seemed taller by a few inches. "I... yes. I do. Why? What do you want?"

Maybe I should've corrected him because it wasn't what *I*

wanted, but the words tumbled out because this situation begged to be saved.

"I'll sign this because you want us to." I nodded to the stack of contracts on his desk. "But you have to come with us to Spain. Say goodbye properly."

Henryk sighed like this moment was taking something out of him, but I was trying to save him. From himself. From his duty. From whatever gave him that sour look and the lines beside his eyes. "Goodbye? But we barely know each other."

"And yet here we are, all together to dissolve a twenty-year marriage." I grinned because his mouth fell open and his eyes went wide. "So, what do you say, Mr. Fancy Pants?"

Henryk lifted his chin, his nose a few inches higher in the air than his snooty attitude had made it a second ago. "I'm too busy for a vacation."

I twirled the pen between my fingers. "Well, I'm not signing until you agree to come with us." I shrugged as if it didn't matter to me, but when Erin nodded and smiled, it mattered a lot to me.

"Blackmail. I figured." Henryk narrowed his eyes.

"It's extortion. So different." I shrugged again. I could do this all day long.

"And I suppose I'll be paying for the whole vacation?"

I shrugged. "I'm happy to hostel my way through Spain, but I don't know if you're quite in shape for backpacking across the country." I was pretty sure Erin wouldn't mind traveling around Europe that way, but the prince's nose wrinkled. His royal stuffiness seemed a bit put off at the idea of sharing a room with ten other people.

"Well?" I raised an eyebrow. The choice was his. He could go on what looked like a much needed getaway and be divorced when he returned home or he could stay here and figure out what to tell his country, his parents and his bride-to-be. "What do you say?"

He nodded suddenly, jerking his head up and down, like nodding was something he was unaccustomed to doing. "Fine. I can rearrange my schedule to accommodate a few days off."

"A week." I wasn't giving this guy a break either. "Seven full days. and don't even think of skipping out on us." It would take us that long to unwind this guy. He was the most uptight person I'd met in years.

Henryk sighed but I sensed he wasn't as put out as he was acting. "Fine."

I stuck out my hand to make sure he didn't back out and smiled when he took it. "Then we have a deal."

"Yes, we do."

I signed the rest of the paperwork and happiness bubbled up from my stomach. Yep, this felt right although I wasn't sure why.

Erin hugged me tightly from behind and I turned to look down at her. "I can't believe we're all going on vacation together."

Her body was all curves and sweetness, and I tugged her closer so I could hold her tighter. "We didn't get a reception or a honeymoon, so a divorce party seems fitting."

She laughed and twisted her arms around my neck to hug me again. I closed my eyes and breathed her in. She was exquisite.

"I don't think divorce parties are meant to be with all your single friends," Erin said, "but I'm not complaining."

I ran my hand over the top of my head, the short hair bristling beneath my palm. "Yeah, well, our marriage was unorthodox, so probably our divorce should be, too."

She smiled up at me and my gaze landed near her lips. God, she was everything a woman should be. So vibrant and happy and sweet. But sweet in a way that made me want to strip her naked and make love to her until neither of us could move.

I clenched my teeth and looked away, breathed out slowly because the images in my head were potent and I needed to slow my roll. Silas met my eyes, and a crooked grin lifted his lips.

Yeah, he knew. Of course, that was because he was as afflicted as I was. No way could he hide it. His face gave away everything. That and those moon eyes he was using to stare at her.

"So, what's the plan?" Silas asked, standing and swiping his hands together. "Do we leave today or are we hanging around the palace until Henryk is ready to come with us?"

We all turned to the prince, who was busy gathering up all the paperwork. "I need at least a day to get everything in line so I can leave." And I could see his mind spinning with possibilities, plans to get out of accompanying us on our vacation. I knew the exact minute he'd come up with something. Fancy Pants smiled. "So, if you'd all like to depart for Spain today, you may. I'll meet you there as soon as I can."

I glanced at Erin and Silas, then shook my head and rolled my eyes before I turned back to Henryk. "I think we should stay and wait for you." I added a smile. "Don't want you getting stuck behind with all your *responsibilities*."

Henryk frowned before glancing down at his briefcase.

That had so been his plan. He was going to send us off, come up with some excuse for why he couldn't leave immediately, and then never show up. And although I should've been happy about his not so covert plan—after all, it was one less guy to share Erin with—a part of me knew that Henryk was a necessary component to whatever was going to happen. And he would've been necessary whether he had the money or not.

"Can we hang around the castle for a day or so?" I asked.

Henryk considered me for a second then tilted his head. "Of course. I will have Francis organize guest suites for you all, and he will book the flights and accommodations, so if you have any special requests, let him know."

"Francis sounds like a handy guy to have around, then."

Henryk huffed and walked to the door. "I need to get these filed, then you'll all receive a copy."

Ray was posted outside the office door, and he moved back when we came into the hallway.

"Raymond, our guests will be staying with us for the night. Take them to Francis. They need rooms and to speak with him. At some point, we'll also need dinner." He didn't say please or thank you, but walked past like the way he spoke was appropriate. And maybe it was, but I had guys who worked for me and I wouldn't ever think to sound so coldly authoritative. I wouldn't have people working for me very long if I behaved so badly.

But this guy just nodded like it was no big deal. "Yes, Sire." Then he turned to us. "I don't believe the palace has ever had this many Americans under our roof." He said it with a smirk, like he was making fun of our nationality. "Let's go find you somewhere to sleep your jetlag off."

His gaze lingered on Erin a moment too long, and annoyance churned in my gut. I cleared my throat, focused on staying calm because she wasn't mine to be jealous over. I'd just signed a paper to make sure of it, and this feeling was wrong. We followed Ray as Henryk disappeared in the other direction.

"Why'd you want him to come with us?" Silas asked quietly as Erin walked beside Ray.

I shrugged. "Not sure. I had a moment. It felt right." The

connection I'd felt to Fancy Pants wasn't something Silas would get right away, and I wasn't in the mood to explain. Hell, I wasn't even sure I could.

Silas shot me a weird side-eye but didn't say more. He knew me well. Knew I did strange things sometimes because my gut told me to. It didn't often lead me astray, so he tended to give me a fair amount of latitude when it came to my gut feelings.

"I was wondering the same thing," Erin said with a look at me over her shoulder. I liked the smile that came with it, so I was over the moon about both and I stumbled and almost fell. Silas grabbed my arm and kept me upright. I nodded my thanks as Erin continued, "If he doesn't want to come with us, why make him?"

"Oh, he wants to," I told her. "He's just so twisted up inside, he couldn't ask. And he sure as hell can't imagine relaxing for a week, that's for sure."

Erin nodded, though she didn't look convinced.

Silas let out a grunt, but his expression turned thoughtful.

We met Francis walking along the corridor toward us, and Ray spoke to him for a moment before he indicated we should follow him. "Come this way."

We did and were shown to bedroom suites the size of apartments. "I'll have all of your luggage brought up so you can settle in."

"Sounds great. Thanks, man." I went in to explore the room allocated to me. Erin said she was just up the hall, and Silas was in the suite next door.

Erin followed me into my room, looking around. "This is pretty much identical to mine. The bathroom's huge, too. Go check it out."

I did, and stood in the middle of the tiled expanse, gaping at all the space. "I've never seen anything this big." And probably wouldn't ever again.

Erin grinned at me, then moved back into my bedroom and sat on my bed. "So, tell me more about you and Silas, Viktor. Do you have girlfriends?"

I laughed and pulled off my shirt, loving the way her eyes ran over my body as I exposed more of my tattoos. Part of me had done that on purpose, to see if she'd choose to look or run away.

"Nah," I said. "We're both single but looking for the right girl."

"Girl? Don't you mean... girls?"

I raised a brow as I answered. "No. I meant girl. Singular." I grinned widely at her, letting that sink in before heading over to the bathroom again. "I need a shower after that long-ass flight. Wanna join me?"

She giggled as she jumped up and hurried over to the door. "I think I'll go call my parents, make sure they know I'm still alive."

She lifted her hand and waved goodbye, and I was left with a body hot and thrumming with desire for the sexy-as-fuck woman I'd just divorced.

CHAPTER 9

Henryk

Anger thrummed through me like the heavy vibration of a guitar string. I'd been hoodwinked into going to Spain with three people I didn't even know.

Okay, so I'd been married to them for twenty years, but that was a farce. An innocent childhood moment that had turned into something with far-reaching ramifications once we all reached adulthood.

What were my parents going to say about me running off to Spain for a week? And how was I going to get out of all my royal commitments?

My stomach roiled with tension as I gave the paperwork to one of the legal team. Tobias, who had been retained by our family for years, notarized the five copies of the divorce papers and kept one for himself before handing the others back. "Thank you," I muttered, clutching the papers.

"Do you need anything else, Your Highness?"

I shook my head and headed to my bedroom, the only place I

seemed to find any peace and quiet these days. I walked into my suite and sat down on my bed, needing a moment to think.

Could I really do this? Go out into the public with three virtual strangers? The press would have a field day if they found out, and any photos taken would be broadcast around for the whole world to see. And probably judge. That would likely include my parents.

There was a knock at the door and when I called out to enter, Raymond walked in. "I was wondering where you were hiding, Henryk. What's going on?"

Raymond was one of the few people who called me by my name rather than title when we were in private. Over the years, he had become a friend of sorts, though he was always professional and respectful when anyone else was around.

I sighed and gave my head of security a rundown on the deal I'd struck with Viktor. It was a fair deal, really. I would have done anything to be released from the strange marriage I'd become tangled up in.

Raymond listened, nodding on occasion, then he unexpectedly burst out laughing.

I glared at him. "It's not funny."

He put a hand to his stomach, still chortling. "Please let me be there when you tell Francis he has to reschedule your whole week. He is going to literally combust!"

I ran a hand through my hair, feeling overwhelmed. Raymond was right. This was a stupid idea.

He walked closer, his face sobering. "If you don't want to go, Henryk, I'm sure I can work out a way to get them to leave without you."

I looked at my friend, a man who'd worked beside me since I'd turned eighteen. "No. I'm a man of my word, though I have to admit I was tempted to pretend I hadn't agreed to it. I've said I'll travel with them for a week, so I will. But I'm just not sure exactly how to do that."

He shrugged. "Easy. You just go. You're the heir to the throne, Henryk. You can do whatever you want."

I pinched the bridge of my nose. "That's not how it works, and you know it, Raymond."

He snorted. "It kinda is how it works, actually. You just don't normally exercise that right. You will have to take me with you, of course. But I wouldn't mind getting a little Spanish sun."

I stood up and shrugged out of my jacket. "You're right. I'll just push aside my obligations..."

"For a more important obligation," he reminded me. "After all, now that you're free to marry Princess Posy, you can do what you want."

I tried not to flinch at that woman's name, but he saw it. I could tell by the knowing look in his eyes.

"Don't say it, Raymond. Don't even say it."

But my head of security had never been one to listen to me when I told him to shut up. At least, not when it was just the two of us. It was something I liked about him. He was genuine, and there were few of those people in my life these days.

"You know you don't have to marry her, Henryk."

I unbuttoned my shirt and threw it onto a nearby couch. "I do. That's not up for discussion. But you're right. One week in Spain could be good. I haven't had a vacation in years."

I couldn't remember the last time I'd taken time off. We didn't take vacations, as such, in my family. My parents were of the view that holidays were an excuse to visit foreign diplomats or do charity work.

"Perhaps Erin could help you forget your responsibilities for an hour or two." Raymond waggled his eyebrows at me suggestively.

I turned away to hide the feelings clogging my chest. "Perhaps." I pulled on a fresh shirt and buttoned the cuffs.

Raymond's phone rang and he excused himself and left to deal with whatever it was that had reared up.

I glanced at my watch. Time for my next meeting. I checked my reflection in the mirror, ran my fingers through my hair to style it neatly once more, then headed off to speak to Francis before returning to the cabinet room.

The conversation with my steward was as uncomfortable as I'd anticipated, but in the end, he conceded to the importance of getting the divorce any way we could, and he agreed to book me on a flight with the other three.

Finally, after more endless and intensely boring meetings, it was time to dress for dinner. I walked to the dining room, where Erin, Silas and Viktor were already drinking wine and chatting happily at the dining table.

"Good evening." I approached the large table and looked down at the pleased faces of my guests. A pang of jealousy ran through me. If only my life were simple enough that I could throw down a few wines and join in their casual laughter.

"Henryk!" Erin grinned up at me.

She was wearing a spaghetti-strap red top with long black trousers, and her hair was down and soft around her shoulders.

"You look beautiful," I said to her, unable to take my eyes off her.

Her cheeks flushed. "Thank you. I really didn't pack for this weather or formal dinners, so my clothing choices are a little limited."

"We didn't either," Silas said with a chuckle.

The two guys wore long-sleeved shirts and no ties, but both looked fit and strong, and I knew whatever they wore, they'd look good.

I inclined my head. "We'll head to Spain in the morning, so you'll all be fine. It'll be me that doesn't have the right clothes for that climate."

I pulled out a chair and sat down with them. There was a bowl of warm rolls and three open bottles of wine.

"I think we need something more substantial than bread," I said, glancing around for the head of hospitality, Neil.

He nodded at my request, hurrying out the door.

"I hope you don't mind that we started without you." Erin sat up straighter in her chair. "Your staff offered us a wine and the next thing we knew, we had three bottles going."

I smiled at her, loving that she had asked. None of my other guests would have bothered to do that.

"Of course not. The wine is there to be enjoyed."

Silas poured wine into my glass, filling it almost to the brim. "You're an hour behind, Henryk. Get drinking. You have to catch up."

"Catch up?" I repeated, picking up my glass and taking a careful sip so I didn't spill the deep red liquid. "I doubt I can do that."

Viktor grinned at me, snatching a bread roll and taking a bite. "Try. You need to loosen up a bit, man."

Although I didn't appreciate the insult in his tone, I kind of agreed with him. I knew I was too uptight, but didn't know how to relax.

I put my mouth to the glass and drank. And then I drank, and drank, and drank some more.

When I set the glass back down, it was empty.

Viktor nodded. "Nice, man."

I shrugged. "You're probably right. If we're going on vacation, why not start right now?"

"Yes!" Silas said, pouring more into my glass, though he didn't fill it up quite as much as last time.

The butler came by with a selection of more wines and I chose three of the best. Part of me wanted to tell them that these wines were meant to be slowly sipped and savored. That each bottle was worth hundreds of dollars. But I kept my mouth shut, not wanting to change the happy, relaxed atmosphere in the room.

"How was your afternoon?" I asked the group.

"I napped," Erin said, meeting my gaze with more warmth than I expected.

"Me, too," Silas said with a laugh. "I lay down on the bed just to see how soft it was, and woke up three hours later."

I turned to Viktor, who took a sip of wine. "I did a bit of work," he said. "Had to check on some business stuff, and found a new project for Silas and me."

"New project?" I asked. "Tell me about that. What do you guys do?"

The food was served, and we spent most of dinner talking about Viktor and Silas's business.

"It sounds like you've both done very well," I said, impressed with their obvious work ethic and ingenuity. For two men who hadn't gone to college and whose parents hadn't been able to help them financially, they'd done extraordinarily well.

"We got lucky on our first project," Silas said, being too modest. "And we've learned a lot over the years."

I looked at Erin, whose face was pink from the wine. "What about you, Erin? Do you enjoy your profession as much as these two?"

She burst out laughing, snorting as well in a cute yet inelegant way. "Oh, definitely not. The more I hang around with these two, the more I'm thinking I need a change."

"What do you mean?" Silas asked.

She sighed heavily. "I don't enjoy my job. I really don't. The pay is decent but climbing the promotion ladder is slow, and I really don't get any joy out of working there. I want to be like you guys. I want to wake up and really look forward to going to work."

Silas reached over and squeezed her hand and she looked up at him with a level of adoration that had me clenching my hand into a fist.

Viktor chuckled beside me, his eyes a little glazed over, due to the wine. "You know, Silas and I killed ourselves laughing when we found out we'd inadvertently gotten ourselves into a poly marriage. A legal one, too."

I frowned at him. "Why?"

"Because we've done a poly relationship before."

"Two, if you count Nancy," Silas added.

I glanced from one guy to the other, and I could see Erin blinking at them too. "You've been in poly relationships before?"

Viktor nodded, his gaze daring me to say anything negative about that fact. "Absolutely. Women need so much love and time and attention. It's a lot easier when you get to share the load with someone else."

Silas chuckled. "Yeah, it definitely works well."

Erin's mouth dropped open. "You guys don't mind sharing one woman? Really? I mean, Viktor said something along those lines earlier, but I thought he was joking."

I was thinking the same thing but didn't want to appear ignorant.

The servants arrived with dessert and Silas reached for a piece of Dreikönigskuchen, a sweet roll filled with citrus rind and raisins.

"We prefer it, actually," Silas answered, after the serving staff had backed away. "It's great fun." He wagged his eyebrows and smiled at Erin.

I nodded as if I knew what he meant and poured myself another glass of wine. *Holy hell.* This conversation had just taken an unexpected turn and I wasn't sure how to get it back on track. Nor was one hundred percent sure I wanted to.

CHAPTER 10

Erin

I stared from one man to the next, and then to the next. Was Henryk agreeing with Silas and Viktor? Or was he too polite to say what he was thinking—which probably matched what I was thinking?

"I can't believe it." I managed to splutter. "That would be like... every woman's dream. You must be overrun with girls applying for the job as your girlfriend."

Silas and Viktor burst out laughing, shaking their heads as though I was joking.

I wasn't.

Being with both of them... at the same time? That would be like paradise!

"No, seriously," I urged.

Silas grinned at me. "Well, no. We don't. Why? Would you like to apply?"

I buried my head in my wine, taking another sip of Dutch

courage before lifting my head and looking him straight in the eye. "It really depends."

The humor disappeared from his expression, but he continued staring at me. "Depends on what?"

"Well," I began, thinking how much I was probably going to regret this conversation in the morning, but pushing on regardless. "Depends on what you mean by dating both of you at once. Like... where would we all sleep? Together? All separate? Or would I bed hop each night?"

My face was literally on fire now, but this was really the part I wanted to know about. Would they have sex with me at the same time, or would I have to choose one or the other?

I glanced over at Henryk, but the prince was cutting up the strange-looking dessert and wasn't looking my way. Probably on purpose, but I didn't care at the moment.

When I looked back to Silas and Viktor, they were staring at each other, but not saying anything out loud. I could almost feel the conversation going on between them.

Finally, Silas looked at me and asked, "What would you prefer?"

Fuck.

How honest did I want to be?

I looked from Silas to Viktor, then back again. "Well, I'd want us all together, I suppose. I mean, I've never done a poly relationship before, but wouldn't it be better to be together? Then no one would miss out."

Silas grinned and Viktor nodded slowly. "Sounds like a plan to me."

I chuckled and reached for some of the cakey roll thing that Henryk had cut up. "Deal."

I glanced from Silas to Viktor, heat surrounding me. I was hot for these guys, and although I didn't see myself falling into bed with them tonight, if there was a chance I could build a relationship with two such amazing men, I'd do it.

I decided that this year was the year the impossible became possible, and with this much wine fuzzing up my brain, I was starting to believe Viktor, Silas and I *was* possible.

My gaze flicked up to the prince, and this time, I caught Henryk looking directly at me. There was an unreadable look in his eyes. "Hey..." I said, not sure what to say to him.

He tilted his head at me. "Hey."

"This conversation must sound very strange to you," I said, starting to ramble out of nerves. "Or maybe it isn't, since poly marriages are common here."

He coughed to clear his throat, a little red creeping up around his neck. "They aren't common, but they are legal."

"For the king as well?" I asked. "Could you do that, too? If you wanted."

Henryk stared at me, his gaze now burning with strong emotion, something I hadn't seen in his eyes before. The wine maybe? I still couldn't read his mood.

"It's not preferred," he hedged.

I narrowed my eyes at him. "But it's not impossible, otherwise this silly, pretend marriage thing we came to undo wouldn't have existed at all. Right?"

Henryk nodded with a jerk of his head.

"Cool." I turned away to focus on the other men, a hot and heavy sense of disappointment in my gut. It was obvious from this conversation that Silas and Viktor would happily start a relationship with me. Henryk... not so much.

I knew I was being unfair. After all, would I happily share one of them with multiple women? No. No, I wouldn't. So why should a man like Henryk share me? Or even *want* me at all, for that matter.

I pushed to my feet, my head spinning and my legs unsteady beneath me. "I think I need to get to bed."

"We'll walk you back to your room." Silas jumped to his feet.

Viktor stood up, then swayed slightly. "Yes. I think we need to call it a night, or tomorrow's flight may be missed."

I nodded and walked toward the door, not bothering to say goodnight to Henryk. I should have, and felt petty for it, so when I opened the door, I turned back to our host with the intent to lift my hand and say goodnight.

But he was there, right in front of me.

"Oh. Wow. You move fast."

Henryk didn't speak. But he slid a hand around my waist, pulled me against his body and kissed me, hard and fast.

When he lifted his head, his eyes were filled with turmoil, but his tone was level when he said, "Goodnight, Erin." And then he turned and walked in the opposite direction from the rest of us.

I stared after him, my mouth half-open and my lips tingling from his kiss.

Viktor chuckled beside me. "Not sure he wants to be left out."

I glanced up at the sexy guy who'd made sure Henryk came with us to Spain. "How come you want him on our vacation?"

Viktor's eyebrows snapped together in question. "What do you mean?"

"I mean... you pushed really hard for him to come. Why?"

He stared down at me with his intense dark gaze. "Not sure, to be honest. I just had a feeling he was needed."

"For me?" I asked, my head starting to spin a little harder the longer I stood there.

"For all of us," Viktor said, offering me his arm, which I gratefully clung to. "Let's get you into bed."

We laughed and stumbled our way down several corridors, got lost, had to ask for help, then finally found ourselves standing in front of my ornate door.

I bumped my shoulder against the wood, staggering. "Do you guys wanna come in?"

Viktor and Silas exchanged glances that I could only interpret as concerned.

"Ah, probably not a good idea " Silas said. "With this much alcohol in us, it doesn't make for good choices."

"You could just sleep with me," I said, smiling up at both of them. "My bed is massive."

Viktor laughed and cupped my chin gently. "Let's all sleep in our own rooms tonight, but once we're in Spain, it's no holds barred. Okay?"

I nodded, a little sad. But at heart, I knew they were right. It was a bad idea to make decisions when I could barely stand up straight. "Okay."

Viktor dipped his head and kissed me softly on the lips. Then Silas did the same thing, lingering a little longer.

"Good night." I managed, before pushing open the door and staggering to the bed.

"Night!" The boys called out before they shut the door behind them.

I didn't bother getting undressed. I just shoved my shoes off and crawled over the big mattress and beneath the covers. Then I lay on my back and stared up at the ceiling, the whole room spinning in a relatively pleasant way.

What a night! I was going to be embarrassed in the morning but for the moment, I could only marvel at the idea that two guys as sexy as Silas and Viktor wanted me. I'd been single forever!

I fell asleep soon after, blissfully happy, and woke many hours later, with a dry mouth and a throbbing head.

"Ah... fuck..." I rolled out of bed to use the toilet, drink two full glasses of water, and take two ADVIL.

Then I passed out again and woke with the sunshine streaming in my window.

I blinked my eyes rapidly, not wanting to get up but realizing too late that I hadn't set an alarm, and we were leaving today.

I jumped out of bed, my stomach lurching as I did.

"Aww... yuck." I reached for my phone, worried I'd be late, but it was barely eight a.m. "Thank God."

I staggered into the bathroom and turned on the shower, hoping I could somehow rehydrate through my skin. "Definitely too much wine. Wayyyy too much wine."

I burped and coughed, and generally groaned at feeling so crappy. But I stripped off my clothes and hopped in the shower, needing to feel better as quickly as possible. The evening came back to me in flashes and I closed my eyes beneath the water spray, wishing my stupidity away.

"Oh my God," I gasped, as one particular conversation came back to me. Had I really organized to date both Viktor and Silas at once?

Had the prince really kissed me, all possessive like that, in front of the other two?

What on earth was going on with me? Everything was so

twisted and upside down. Me, who couldn't even find a single guy to date, now had three amazing men kissing me at once! *Wow.*

I finished my shower and managed to dry my hair, take more ADVIL and get dressed.

By the time nine o'clock rolled around, I was mostly packed and ready.

There was a knock at the door and when it opened, one of the male servants stood there. "Good morning, Miss Wright. I've been sent for your luggage. The car to the airport leaves shortly."

I nodded. "Yes. Here you go." I gestured to the suitcases on the bed. "Thank you."

He took my bags and I gathered up the last of my personal things into my satchel then said goodbye to the most amazing suite I'd ever stayed in. "I might see you again soon." I told my extremely comfortable bed.

I was being a little too optimistic to think I'd ever be allowed back to stay at the palace again, but it was a nice thought. I shut my door and made my way toward the dining room, my stomach twisting with hunger and expressing its need for a greasy hamburger.

CHAPTER 11

Henryk

Waking up with a hangover and the knowledge that I had to climb on a plane in a few hours was not pleasant. Quite the opposite.

The misery was made even greater by the fact that I was woken by my personal cell phone ringing. That meant it could only be one of a very short list of people who was trying to call me.

"Hello?" I spoke into the phone, my voice unexpectedly husky and groggy—no doubt from all the very expensive wine I'd drunk last night.

"Henryk. What's wrong with you?"

I closed my eyes and rolled over to lay my head on the pillow once more. "Good morning, Mother."

"What's this I hear about you going on a vacation? You're not scheduled to travel to Spain at all this year."

Fucking Francis told on me.

I tried not to sigh too loudly but enough of the sound escaped that my mother heard.

"Henryk!"

I wasn't a playboy prince. I didn't get vacations. I got "scheduled" time off, occasionally, when we had diplomatic visits in exotic countries. That was the extent of my free time.

"Mother, the only way I could get those papers signed was to agree to go on this vacation with them." I rubbed my eyes and forced myself to sit up, cursing those last few glasses of wine. They'd really put me over the edge.

Even so, I didn't regret kissing Erin. Not for one second. I only wished...

"Henryk." My mother's tone was annoyed.

"Mother, this was your play. No entanglements. It's what you said. I'm untangling so I can marry your princess. Isn't that what you want?" I hadn't said it out loud much in the past, as secretly I'd railed against the planned marriage.

But after reaching a level of loneliness I'd never before experienced, I changed my mind.

"You've decided?" she asked, breathless with whatever emotion she was feeling.

I'd never been able to really understand or interpret my mother very well. Although in this instance, it was fairly obvious she wanted a son and a prince who bowed to her wishes and did what she said without complaint.

"Yes, Mother. I'll marry the princess." And hopefully have a few children and find some happiness outside of fulfilling my duty.

"That's wonderful news, Henryk. Enjoy your vacation and we will see you when you return."

She disconnected the call and I swung my legs over the side of the bed and sat up. Today was going to be interesting. I was leaving for a vacation without any work commitments with three strangers—one of whom I wanted to get into bed as soon as possible.

I groaned and hauled myself into the shower before ringing the bell for my valet. He packed my bags while I got dressed and headed to the dining room for a light breakfast. The hangover breakfast, to be exact, of toast and water. Only toast and only water.

Silas, Viktor and Erin were already at the table, but they weren't speaking. They were all pale, not a bright morning eye among them.

I chuckled and the sound made the ache in my head more of a throb. "Everyone re-thinking that last bottle of wine?"

"The last one?" Erin groaned.

"More like the last two," Silas said, reaching for a glass of orange juice and a piece of toast.

I sat down in my seat and poured a coffee. "I changed our plane itinerary slightly."

Erin sighed. "I hope you moved the flight to tomorrow?"

I chuckled at the hope in her tone. "No. But instead of using the commercial airline, we're taking my private plane."

Silas lifted his head. "You have a private plane?" He cocked his head and then nodded. "Of course, you have a private plane. You're going to be the king." Then he looked seriously at me. "Do you fly it, too?"

I grabbed a glass of water and popped some painkillers. *Americans.* "God, no. I have no aspirations to become a pilot. I'm not Christian Grey."

Erin burst out laughing, but the guys just stared at me in confusion.

I met Erin's eyes and grinned. "At least you got it."

She nodded and we ate in silence for a while, then Ray entered the dining room, dressed in casual jeans and a fitted, black shirt.

"Good morning, all."

His tone was cheery, not the least bit hung over. We all groaned in unison, the song of overindulgence.

Ray chuckled and walked around the side of the table to stand next to Erin. "Drink a little too much last night, did we?"

She stared up at him. "Oh, yeah. Definitely not the way to start a vacation."

Ray glanced down at his watch. "The plane leaves in a few hours, which means we should start heading toward the cars. The private airport is about an hour out of town."

A stupid oversight on my behalf. The commercial airport was closer.

"Are you coming with us, Ray?" Erin asked, glancing from me to my security guard and back again.

Ray tilted his head and smiled at her—only at her. "Of course."

"Of course?" Silas repeated, pulling himself to a stand, panting like it took everything in him to get to his feet. "Why of course?"

"Because he's my personal security," I explained.

Silas wrinkled his nose. "Really? You don't really look like security." Then he gave Ray a once-over that only a man with a death wish would think was appropriate.

I got to my feet too. It was time to leave. "Thus, his appeal."

"Don't worry, Silas," Ray said with a sly smile. "I won't cramp your style."

"Just keep your clothes on," I told Ray with a glare before

turning to the others and explaining, "Ray tends to hog all the attention at the beach, pool, or wherever you are."

Erin got to her feet, unstable, tumbling into Ray, who steadied her.

She stared up at him. "You know, you look more like Henryk's personal shopper."

A laugh burst out of Ray, a man who didn't laugh. Hell, he'd very rarely smiled until Erin got here. Now his grin might well have been painted on his face for as often as he was flashing the damned thing. "I'll take that as a compliment."

She grinned. "You should."

I wasn't quite sure how "personal shopper" could be taken as a compliment for a man with as many skills as Ray, but I didn't bother questioning it any further. I just followed the others out of the dining room, along the hallway and into the car waiting for us outside the front entrance.

The four of us slipped into the back of the stretch limo, while Ray chose to sit up front with the driver.

"Anyone need any ADVIL?" Erin asked, holding out a white bottle.

Both guys nodded, took the tablets and washed them down with some water from bottles on offer in the limo.

Erin was sitting next to Silas, whose neck tattoo caught my eye. He looked like a guy you wouldn't want to meet in a dark alley at night, or so the saying went.

"How many tatts do you have?" I asked him.

Silas met my gaze and ran his hand over his buzz cut in an already-familiar way. "A few. Why?"

"Only wondering," I said with a shrug. "Just trying to make conversation."

"How many do you have?" Silas countered.

I shook my head, "None." I'd always wondered what it'd be like to get a tattoo. But it wouldn't be considered very princely, I was sure. And since I was photographed everywhere, including at the beach and in my own backyard, there wasn't much hope in hiding them, no matter where I put one.

"Well, if we're making conversation, can I ask *you* something?" Silas said.

I nodded. "Of course." I was a master at avoiding questions I didn't want to answer. Part of international diplomacy.

"Viktor and I are going to pursue Erin."

She looked up at that and shot both of us a shy grin.

"Try out a poly relationship again, but for keeps," Silas added. "Do you want in on that?"

He couldn't have surprised me more if he'd reached over and punched me in the face. "Ah... well... that's an interesting question." My face flushed with heat and probably color. To buy some time, I grabbed for a bottle of water and took a large swig.

"It's a lot. Requires ground rules. Take some time Think about it," Silas said, nodding and glancing away.

He then slid his hand over Erin's thigh and took hold of her hand.

Jealousy roiled in my gut, piercing me with pain. I coughed to clear my throat. I didn't want to commit to anything, but I also didn't want to be excluded. "I don't think making a commitment either way would be smart at this point in time."

Erin glanced up at me. "You're getting married, Henryk. I don't want to..." She shook her head then looked down at her hands. She was out of words, and I couldn't help because I couldn't think about anything other than the prospect of being with her.

Viktor punched me gently in the arm. "Tell us about the chick your parents are forcing on you."

I forced a smile to my lips. I barely knew the woman and didn't have a lot of information to share. "She's a princess from the Morovian royal family. She's been brought up understanding the responsibilities of being a royal, and she will be a very suitable wife."

Viktor nodded. "Yeah... she sounds hot."

I rolled my eyes and but couldn't help laughing. "Oh, that's what you want to know, is it? Hang on a moment." I pulled out my cell phone and found some recent images of my betrothed, attached to a media article. "Here you go."

I handed the phone over and Viktor flicked through the article. "She's really cute."

"She is."

"Then what's the problem?" Viktor asked.

"Problem?" Oh, but let me count the ways, the number of problems. Tabloids. Rumors.

"Yeah." Viktor ran his hand through his hair. "You don't look excited or happy about it."

I smiled at him, but even to me it felt fake. Probably looked more like a grimace. "There's no problem except for the fact that I'm about to be staring at you three going at it all week."

"We invited you to join in." Silas lifted Erin's hand up to kiss her fingers. Erin stared at me as he did so, and my stomach fluttered in a strange way.

I glanced out the window to try and take some of the heat out of my glare because at that point in time, I wanted to skewer Silas with a sword.

When I finally spoke, my voice was clipped. "We'll be at the airport soon and we can all rest for the flight."

Would it be like this every time one of those *construction workers* touched her? No way was I going to survive a week of this. But my word was my word, and that was all there was to it.

Erin

Apparently, those with private planes, even in public airports, aren't bothered by security measures. We were whisked through the airport and across the concourse to our gate—a private gate at the end of the terminal. And then we were ushered down a flight of steps to the tarmac.

Henryk had said he had a private plane. I couldn't say exactly what I'd pictured—probably something out of the movie *Pearl Harbor*, massive and clunky. But whatever I'd been thinking, it was nothing like what was waiting for us.

A jet by any other name was still a jet, but this thing was sleek and shiny. It looked more like a giant needle with wings. It had a row of windows down the side extending from the stairs waiting for us and past the wings to the tail fin. And no, I didn't know if that was its official name, but that was what I was calling it.

Inside, the plane was like the castle but with wings. Opulent and lush. There was carpet and gold plating. *Gold plating.* A rim of it around the windows, at the edge of the tables, along the top of a drinks cart that had gold-trimmed decanters full of what would likely be top-notch and alcohol—even though I had no idea what kind.

In the whole flying tube of greatness, there wasn't a single nick. Not in the plastic, nor the wood, or even the drinks cart that appeared affixed to absolutely nothing.

The act of walking onto this plane was, in itself, a *holy crap* moment. Even the stairs were carpeted and they belonged to the airport, which meant that the Lichtenstein royal family had their own set of stairs reserved for their use. That was some serious pull.

I lifted my head, acting regal because the moment demanded it. Also because it was easier to catch my breath without all the slouching and slumping my normal posture demanded.

After a quick glance around, noting more gold accents—gold seatbelts, for heaven's sake—I took the window seat near the middle of the plane. I thought that since there was a chair next to me and two facing mine, it left room for all of us to sit together.

"Nice place you got here, fancy pants," Viktor said, a smirk in his voice but not on his face.

"You would rather fly Atlantic coach?" Henryk cocked an eyebrow and it was adorable. Of course, at this point, I hadn't seen much about him that wasn't adorable.

Viktor ignored him and Henryk wasn't having it.

He went on, "Pretend it's a park. You'll be fine."

Uh-oh. Some of Henryk's sparkly princely charm was in danger now. Viktor looked like he was one word away from knocking it off him, and with the smarminess that had just come out of the prince's mouth, I wouldn't blame Viktor one bit.

But Viktor didn't hit him. Instead, he took the seat next to mine rather than one across from me. Henryk's scowl immediately deepened, and Viktor smiled for the first time.

Oh, yeah. This isn't uncomfortable. At all.

Silas sat across from Viktor and me, so Henryk sat on the opposite side of the plane, which felt a little strange, seeing as how he was our host on this plane. Even though he tried to hide behind the screen of his laptop, I could see him watching me, and yet pretending like he wasn't. I liked the feeling of it—the awareness that sizzled between us.

But with my attention on Henryk, I was ignoring Viktor and Silas. I didn't want that either, so I focused back on my American boys. "So, construction? HGTV happen to you or did you two happen to it?"

Silas chuckled. "I like a witty girl."

I waggled my eyebrows at him. "You found one." I liked to think so, anyway. At least, sometimes.

"It's about building something from nothing. There's an enjoyment in seeing the finished product and knowing we did it." Viktor grinned, and looked at me with such pride in his eyes, I couldn't help returning his smile wholeheartedly.

"Unless it's restoring something to its former glory," Silas added. "That feels pretty spectacular, too."

"They're like Laurel and Hardy." The snarky comment came from across the aisle. I liked that Henryk was trying to be a part of the conversation, but it was clear he didn't quite know how to join in. Had no one ever told him how to converse with a group of friends? I wasn't familiar with the reference and Viktor's raised eyebrows said he wasn't, either.

Silas frowned. "Is that a jab, pretty boy?"

Ray chuckled from where he sat across from Henryk. I craned

my neck to see around Viktor and raise an eyebrow at him. Ray wiped the smile from his face and held up the obligatory hand of silent apology.

"Who the hell are Laurel and Hardy?" I asked. At least we could safely assume they were people. Henryk wouldn't have the audacity to compare Viktor and Silas to horses or something, would he?

"They're a comedy team," Henryk explained.

"Were we being funny?" Silas asked, his eyebrows pulling together.

He'd been talking about a subject he felt passionate about. Being compared to a comedy team wasn't endearing.

Silas went on to add, "I didn't mean to be funny and I don't think Vik meant to, either."

"Nope. Not funny at all. We genuinely enjoy what we do for a living." Viktor shot a glare at Henryk.

The words hung in the air, unspoken. *Do you, Henryk? Do you enjoy being a prince?*

"It wasn't meant to be an insult. They just have a lot of back and forth and you two reminded me of them." Henryk typed on his computer and pulled up a picture of two guys—one big with a Hitler-style mustache and the other skinny with a giant forehead. Both had funny hats and bowties. Not mirror images of Viktor and Silas, that was for sure.

This conversation had passed awkward and was now heading somewhere bad. Henryk was ruining this vacation before it had even started, so I stepped in and tried to placate everyone.

"Guys... I'm certain he didn't mean... that." I pointed at the small screen across the aisle.

"Of course, I meant it." Henryk's brow pinched as though he didn't understand he was being rude.

I only got to stare in disbelief at him for a second before Viktor nudged me.

"What is with this guy? Showing off his money and rubbing our noses in it. Then calling us low-class and comparing us to badly-dressed comedians." Viktor looked directly at me. "Is that how *you* see us?"

"No, not at all," I reassured him.

But it was obvious he wasn't listening to me. Nor was Silas. They were one word from chest thumping while they grunted. Henryk too, probably.

I tried again. "Come on, guys. I'm sure Henryk didn't mean anything by it." I glanced at him and if he didn't change expression soon, he was going to be stuck with a permanent scowl. "Right, Henryk?"

"Of course, I didn't mean anything, and I'm not rubbing anyone's nose in anything, either." He rolled his eyes as though to prove a point.

I could've told him that eyerolling wasn't the kind of move to indicate sincerity, but he didn't ask and I wasn't interjecting just now. I wanted to see the three guys work it out by themselves. Plus, if things got physical, Ray would be there to break it up.

"I'm rich. I can't help that." Henryk shrugged. "I'm sharing with you. What more do you want from me?"

He was incredible and beautifully so, but again, I'd yet to find anything he didn't do like a GQ model.

Viktor wasn't about to be put off by the fact that Henryk looked the way he did. Anger flashed in his eyes, and his jaw was tightening and flexing like it was doing reps. Obviously, big blue eyes didn't matter to him.

I sighed. We were still barreling toward an ugly confrontation. I only hoped Ray had a plan, because if someone got thrown out the emergency door of the plane, it was really going to put a dampener on the rest of our vacation.

"Laurel and Hardy were a comedy team from the silent film era," Henryk said after the silence went on way too long. "They were Americans and quite famous. Paved the way for Abbott and Costello." Henryk was losing his audience, quick. "You know. Who's on first?"

"Better check him, Erin. I think he's having a stroke. He's muttering random words now." Silas was getting in on the "Hate Henryk" act.

I groaned and leaned my head back on the pillowed headrest behind me. "Maybe we should all rest. I've heard that you need a lot of rest to do Spain the right way."

Oh, God. If that was the best I could do to stop them bickering, we weren't going to make it through a whole week. Likely not even the first twenty-four hours.

"Yeah. Maybe." Henryk twisted the laptop toward him and typed, slapped the enter button and shot a glare at Viktor while he waited for his page to load.

Silas crossed his arms and looked out the window to his left. Viktor huffed next to me and shot withering glances across the aisle, that had absolutely no effect on Henryk.

Now I know why assigned seats are a good idea.

CHAPTER 13

Silas

Whoa.

It was legit the only word I could think of until the word "swank" came to mind. I'd thought the plane was lit, but this resort was... whoa.

Ibiza. I'd heard of it. I'd watched some reality TV show set here. But damn.

Erin had a brochure in her hand that some random concierge had shoved at her and she was reading while Pretty Boy's bodyguard or BFF or whatever, checked us in.

Erin's voice was bubbling with excitement. "We can start the day with yoga on our private deck, slide into breakfast, take a ride on the ocean. We can mountain bike and hike, learn to cook... we can do *everything* here. Wow! This is so amazing!"

I wasn't sure about the other two guys, but my idea of *everything* in relation to Erin had nothing to do with hiking or biking. And yoga was definitely not a sport I planned to indulge in unless she counted downward doggy-style.

I chuckled to myself because no one else was in my head to hear the joke.

Instead of sharing my internal monologue with anyone, I watched Erin instead. She was a siren, a woman with some incredible magic. Probably something cooked up by that little Merlin dude with the glasses and... never mind.

"What's a SUP?" She spoke up, a small frown crinkling between her brows.

Looking to me for the answer was probably a mistake. I was by no means stupid but I had a feeling she wasn't talking about the short version of "What's up". I gave a cool-guy wink, a pair of finger pistols and then a shrug because I had no clue what she was talking about.

"It's a Stand-up Paddle Tour." If nothing else, we could count on Pretty Boy to translate rich people talk into stuff we understood.

"Ooh. Let's do that. Can we book in a SUP, Ray?" She looked at the assistant and he nodded as a slow smile slid across his face.

"I'll set it up."

Of course, he would. He would probably set up whatever she wanted. He seemed to be wrapped around her little finger already.

I wondered for a second how I could get on the list of her secret desires. In fact, I wanted to be a lot more than just a desire. I wanted to be one of her needs.

Henryk stood at the counter speaking in what sounded like perfect Spanish. Of course. I didn't like that guy.

I looked at Viktor. "No way can we afford this place."

"Moneybags is paying." Viktor nodded to where the prince of perfection was smiling at the desk clerk like he was offering to buy her a car. Hell, I couldn't speak Spanish, so for all I knew, he was.

"His name in Henryk, guys," Erin added, with a roll of the eyes.

I shrugged at her. "Who cares?"

His attitude on the plane said, "*I don't care about anyone*," but his smile was the *come-get-me* version and Erin was eating it up. She might've even batted her lashes a time or two. I was a little bit jealous, I had to admit. He oozed charm. All I could offer was muscle.

We'd agreed to share, but I wasn't sure how easy that was going to be.

"I care," Erin said. "And honestly, if he's good enough to pay for this trip, maybe we should be a little respectful?" Her voice was soft rather than confrontational, but her words packed a punch. Then she glanced at him over her shoulder and I saw that look in her eyes.

Oh, boy.

Whether or not we liked this guy wasn't the issue. The fact was, Erin liked him. And she was right. Since he was paying for this party palace, maybe we could find some common ground other than just the girl we all liked. It was a thought, anyway.

"It's cool that he's paying," I managed to choke out.

I wished we could afford to stay here without him. But we couldn't, and that was a fact.

Henryk was still at the counter. Unless that desk clerk was the new fiancée, I couldn't imagine what they were still talking about. It sure as hell didn't look like he was haggling—I would've been. She was all smiles, and he was grinning like a fool. For all I knew, he was trying to pick her up. Not that I cared. Actually, I did care a little. I hoped he was. Less competition for Erin.

If he wanted to diddle the help, that left more time with Erin for me and Vik. And it didn't bother me to call that woman the help, because I, too, was the help. I liked the role myself. It gave me purpose. More so than wearing my crown around the castle all day, anyway.

But Henryk didn't go off with the other chick. He walked back over to us with a bunch of key cards in his hands. He handed them out and I frowned. Of course, he was going to take the room next to hers. He probably didn't even have a fucking room. He probably had a whole suite. Hell, maybe the whole floor? "Why do you get to decide who gets what room?"

He chuckled a little, looked at me like I was the one with the nerve to ask, then shook his head. "Well, I gave them out randomly, so I'm not even sure which one is which. But I am paying, so I should have the suite I want."

"Silk sheets, satin pillows?" I pushed closer to stand next to him. I outweighed him by a few pounds, and was taller by a few inches. And I wanted him as aware of it as I was that his bank account had six more zeroes than mine.

The smarmy prick smirked. "You probably don't know this, but silk sheets are a bitch to sleep on."

"I wouldn't know that?" My blood was on fire with the need to pound this prick to a pulp. "Why the fuck wouldn't I know it? Rich bastards like you aren't the only ones who've slept with a woman on silk sheets." I gave him a shove.

He pushed me back, and then before he got his royal ass kicked in a lobby full of people, the security servant stepped in. He pushed his employer back and away from me, then stood in front of him.

"Get out of the way." I wasn't about to let this guy—prince or not—treat me like a pauper.

"Maybe you should all go to your rooms and cool off. Maybe have a nice, calming nap," the security guy said.

I didn't like this jerk's attitude, either.

I scoffed because I didn't need to be told by anyone that I'd missed my little nap. But fuck, that guy had a very well-defined chest. I didn't normally notice those things, but his shirt was tight, and that made it obvious. His shoulders were broad and his pecs were a little too defined.

I wasn't a slouch in the workout department, but this dude probably could've given me a run for my money. He was a walking contradiction. Being so buff, but dressed like a department store mannequin. He was pretty and gelled and moussed and coiffed.

But right now, I didn't give a damn. Mr. Muscles was standing between me and the prince's ass kicking—an ass kicking he had coming, and would undoubtedly happen at some point before this week was up. If he didn't pull his head in and stop with the snide me-rich-boy-you-poor-boy attitude.

Prince Pretty Boy nodded toward a waiting bellman. "Shall we?"

Erin grabbed my arm, pulling my attention down to her. "Yes. Can we go see our rooms?"

She left the question hanging as though I was the only thing standing between her and the vacation of her dreams.

I nodded and managed to curb my anger enough to follow along with the plan.

The bellman led us to a bungalow block. It turned out Henryk had booked four separate sleeping rooms with locked doors on each side and stairs that led to a common area below, a private deck and an infinity pool. I could sure as hell get used to this life of luxury.

I should've taken that moment to thank the prince, and I would, soon. But it was going to have to wait until I cooled off; until I didn't want to whoop his ass anymore.

Swank wasn't just a word. It was a lifestyle, and for the next seven days, I was living it.

* * *

Erin

This was so not the way I wanted to spend the next three weeks of my life. Dodging conflict left and right. It would ruin our ability to have fun together.

I glanced at Ray, who smiled and slung an arm around my shoulders, pulling me in to his rock-hard side. "You've started quite the pissing contest, young lady."

Like I didn't know. "Yeah."

He laughed, then dropped his voice to a whisper. "If I wasn't gay, I would date you myself and let all the silly children sulk in their playpens. But you, my sweet, are going to have to work this one out without me." His smile was smug as hell.

Gay, huh? That explains the hot body and awesome clothes.

I couldn't help but smile back because he was right. He was the kind of guy who was always right, but it was easy for him when he didn't have skin in the game.

"Now's as good a time as any, I suppose." Better to get it out of the way before it turned into a full-on hell week.

He nodded and went to the door of Henryk's suite. The prince had disappeared inside as soon as we entered the common area and it took a while after Ray knocked for him to open the door again.

Ray spoke quietly to him and I watched Henryk for a reaction. To his credit, he didn't roll his eyes or mutter or scoff. Instead, he smiled and nodded at Ray, shut the door behind himself and walked into the generous living area.

He sat on one couch—there were two pristine white sofas facing each other—and waited. I took the spot next to him this time, because the others had ganged up on him on the plane. I wanted to show them that I had Henryk's back the same as I would one of theirs if they needed it.

But Viktor had been the one to invite Henryk along in the first place. In fact, he'd blackmailed him into coming, because he'd said Henryk was lonely. He knew. Could see it.

That was all well and good, but now, Viktor was acting like Henryk had done something wrong by paying for the trip, by flying us here in his private plane, and by putting us up in this paradise of a hotel. And Silas was apparently a master of the dirty look. At least that was how it seemed every single time Henryk spoke. Or breathed. Or talked.

This needed to stop. I'd had enough of the childish behavior.

Henryk glanced down at me and smiled and there was something softer and sweeter this time in his expression, than there had been on the journey here.

I waited for Viktor and Silas to enter the common area.

Ray sat in a chair behind the sofa Henryk and I were seated on. He had a view of the ocean on one side and the TV on the other. Between our sofas was a smokeless firepit, but we didn't have it lit. Sun streamed in the windows and reflected off the water outside. The view was stunning.

When the other two joined us and sat on the couch opposite us, I speared them with a stern look. "I wanted to make this clear to the three of you. I don't like all this anger." And because this wasn't my first rodeo with angry men, I smiled, but made it a pouty kind of smile that usually worked. "Can't we all get along?"

"I don't like their insinuations," Henryk said, and in his accent *insinuations* was one sexy word. "I'm not rubbing anyone's nose in my money. I'm trying to provide what I can to make this a nice trip for you all."

I knew that. He wasn't showing off. He had what he had, and he was kindly letting us benefit from it. I could also see how the others would think he was trying to buy his way in. But they were the ones who'd asked him to come along. He was the one making sure they were comfortable and had luxury accommodations.

Viktor looked at Henryk. "We aren't insinuating anything." Then he sighed and looked at Silas, who raised his eyebrows and shrugged.

Silas would go along with whatever Viktor said. I knew that it wasn't because he was a follower. They'd probably sat in the room earlier and discussed how they were going to handle everything, before they arrived in the common area.

Silas looked at me and smiled, but when he looked at Henryk, a shadow crossed over his face. "Look, I was a bit out of line earlier. It's good of you to pay for all this, Henryk. But man, it's tough to accept. It's intimidating to be sitting here in a suite paid for by someone else, knowing we're already a step down because we can't afford to give Erin anything like this."

To his credit, Henryk didn't flinch. "Well," he said, his fingers tapping on his thighs as he considered Silas's words. "I can give her luxury, but I can't give her all you guys can." He looked down at the empty fire pit. "I can't be easy and relaxed. I can't laugh or joke around as easily as you two. I don't even really know how, to be honest. There's a weight on my shoulders. And it's… heavy."

He looked back and forth between Silas and Viktor as if willing them to understand. I rested a hand briefly on his bicep and squeezed gently. He took a deep breath and let it out slowly.

Viktor shook his head. "Not this week, my friend. This week, you aren't Henryk, Prince of Lichtenstein with that heavy weight on your shoulders. This week you're just Henryk, a guy who might or might not share his time and his bed with the most beautiful woman this side of the sky." *Oh, I like that last bit*!

I grinned at him. He might've been saying it to Henryk, but he was saying it *for* me. And I wanted to thank him, but first, they had to work everything out. In this, I was but a bystander. And as much as I wanted to help, I couldn't.

"I can't just pretend I'm not who I am," Henryk said, sounding confused.

I pressed my lips into a thin line so I didn't laugh. It wasn't as existential as it sounded. He really was a prince, and he was in line to take his country's throne. Forgetting that for one day or one hour or one minute, was probably as difficult for him as it was for us to forget that he was a prince. I certainly hadn't been able to stop thinking about it for very long. Especially here, surrounded in every direction by reminders of his lifestyle.

He looked at me. Not a sidelong glance, not anything in passing, but a solid, long gaze, his eyelids at half-mast, his lips slightly parted. "Are you sorry you came to Lichtenstein? Sorry we're all here now?"

I was no novice or young virgin. I knew what we were here for, and I wanted them. I wanted them more than anything. I wanted to be worshipped and devoured and cherished. What woman didn't want that? I was just aiming for things on the grander scale. It scared me, but the idea of being in a sexual relationship with all three of these men was the most exciting thing I'd ever considered before in my life.

Who knew that when this all started, I would end up in Ibiza with the same three boys I'd "married" as a child on a playground in Washington DC? I certainly didn't. But, as I looked at each one now, I couldn't believe my luck.

"No. I'm not sorry at all." I moved my hand from Henryk's arm to his thigh. "Have fun with us, Henryk. Let it all go. Just for a few days. Here, no one knows you."

He laughed. "I'm a prince. Your words can't change that."

"Not here. Here you're just a guy in a baseball cap and sunglasses who's on vacation like the rest of us." I wanted this, I really did. Whatever it turned out to be, I wanted us all to give this a real chance. I'd heard everything that they'd said in the castle before we left. I'd heard it all. I'd trembled like a virgin before her first time.

In a way I was innocent to this sort of love, but that was as tantalizing as any other thought or idea I'd ever had. And no way in hell was I passing up the chance that was in front of me.

As Henryk slowly began to nod, I relaxed beside him. I shot all three of them a wide grin and, after a moment, they all smiled back at me. "So, how about dinner? I'm starved." I figured that was as good a place to start as any.

CHAPTER 14

Erin

Dinner was gourmet because, *of course*. Five-star gourmet. Mediterranean food and good company. There wasn't a lot more a girl could ask for.

Henryk and Viktor sat across from me and this time, Silas sat beside me. They were all in button-downs and jeans. Man-cologne wafted the air, and I liked it. What I didn't especially enjoy was the oddity of the dinner.

It wasn't odd because I was sitting with three very gorgeous men. It was odd because every time one of them looked at me, another one shot the looker a glare.

The tension was thick, and the silence was loud. "Dinner's delicious," I tried at one point. *Holy crap.* It was a feeble attempt. And no one spoke in reply, which made my need to fill the silence all the stronger. Our little pre-dinner talk had seemed to work in part, but obviously it had done nothing to fix the awkwardness between the guys.

"Yummmm," I said, spiking up a piece of flaky pastry and loading it into my mouth.

No one answered or did more than scrape their silverware along the plate to create that horrible screeching sound. I set down my fork, adjusted it so it was parallel to my knife on the other side of my plate, then I arranged my wine glass so that the stem was a perfect three-inch distance from the rim of my plate. And then when everything was perfectly perfect, I looked up.

They were all engrossed with their food and their plates and their scraping forks. I slapped my hand on the table. Hard. When they looked up, I stared at each one of them slowly. Viktor with his quick sparkling smile. Henryk with the big, blue eyes. Silas with the shoulders I wanted to cling to. But their attitudes were dragging me down.

I looked at my plate. It was a shame to waste the rest of such an artful looking meal, but my stomach clenched. I couldn't take this stress. I pushed it away too hard and Silas saved my wine before it toppled over, too. I took the glass from his hand. Then I took a big sip of the wine to fortify my nerves before I spoke.

"Guys, we have to talk."

No way was I going to suffer through a week of tension-filled silence. This was supposed to be a vacation, filled with hours of sun, soaking and fun. I waited until all the forks were down and I had their undivided attention.

"Look, I don't pretend to understand the ways of men." I pointed another look at each of them. "But I can't do this for an entire week." I already had a headache and the week had barely started. "The tension in here is on a whole other level and while I'm all about a poly relationship with you guys, I don't need all this." I waved a hand and narrowed my eyes. "It's too much."

They nodded. Every single one of them, but no one spoke. No one offered a resolution to the problem. In fact, there was so much blank staring I was tempted to snap my fingers in front of their faces just to make sure they were still in there.

"We have a problem, and I don't think we can leave it to resolve itself. There's just too much..." I didn't know how to describe it. "Weight in the air."

I didn't seem to have anyone's attention. They were too busy hating each other and not listening to me.

I was busy glaring and grunting. Not really grunting, but groaning was close.

Silas laid his hand over mine on the right side of my plate, so of course, Henryk reached across the table so he could hold my left hand and then Viktor huffed and puffed hard enough to blow my house down.

I pulled my hands out from the guys' grasps and into my lap. Then I nodded. This was exactly what I was talking about. And now I was the one huffing and puffing like the big, bad wolf. It wasn't conscious, and as soon as I caught myself making those sounds, I quit doing it. Fast. Mostly because it sounded borderline pornographic, and that wasn't the kind of mood I wanted to convey just at that moment.

When I looked up again, the guys weren't capitulating. Instead, the scowls were deeper, the glares more narrowed and darker.

I picked up my fork and shoved another bite of food between my lips, fuming and cursing in my head. There was no call for this behavior. I wasn't a toy for them to fight over.

I looked at Silas. He glanced back and smiled, but as soon as he turned to Henryk, he sneered. It was the same with Viktor and when Henryk looked at either of them, animosity flashed across his features. There was no one I'd ever seen who could do animosity quite like Henryk. Must've been the royal blood.

But this was a lot for one person to have to wade through. How could I make them stop?

"Listen, guys, this is three times the testosterone I'm used to. Three times the machismo. Three times the masculinity. And I don't want to call it toxic, but I'm about ten seconds away from calling for a Hazmat suit."

They all stared at me as if suddenly shocked.

So, now I knew that the conversational threshold for their attention was the almost off-handed mention of Hazmat. And that did not amuse me one bit.

"Toxic?" Silas was the first to speak.

Henryk looked at him. "It means that she thinks we're—"

"I know what it means."

Silas's snap was a precise example of exactly what I was talking about and I jerked to my feet before shooting him a look—*the* look, the one that said I wasn't amused. It involved a cocked eyebrow and lips pinched into a cupid's bow of annoyance. The *piece de resistance,* the thing that held the look together, was the nostril flare, and I turned my head at each of them so they could see it clearly.

They all stood, because even though their walks of life were different, they were all gentlemen.

"My point is..." I spoke slowly, with a deliberate pause for another flared nostril glance at each of them. "That you guys are missing the mood of this vacation and quite frankly, you're making it uncomfortable for me." Not fair, I wanted to add, but didn't. "We could all split up and go our separate ways, but that would ruin everything this vacation was meant to be about, so I'm out of suggestions. Other than calling it a day. I'm not a toy for you all to fight over."

No one spoke. Then, as if on cue, all three of them looked down, and suddenly, I was being outshone by silverware and plates. Figuratively and literally.

I rolled my eyes. They were either not listening or they didn't care. Either way, I was too insulted to do more than shove my chair all the way back and step away from the table.

"I'm going to bed. I have a headache and jetlag and I think we need a little more 'go with the flow' and a little less angry faces before tomorrow or I'll be the one who doesn't want it to work and you will be the ones ruining something I've wanted to do for my entire life." I said it all in one sentence and without much more than a sigh to punctuate the end.

Then, because I was inspired by my own courage at speaking up, I decided to show them what I meant, rather than just tell. I turned to Silas, wrapped my hand around the back of his neck and pulled him down. His lips parted, probably in surprise, but I didn't care.

His mouth was warm and soft, and I slipped my tongue between his full lips and kissed him until he took over, cradled my face between his hands and deepened the kiss. Then because I was a believer in leaving before they tired of me, I broke the kiss.

I didn't dare meet any of their gazes, because I didn't want to see what any of them were thinking. This was going to happen my way and in my time. Period. I was sick of their petty bickering.

Then I walked around the table to Henryk. He was about the same height as Silas and he was easily as kissable. His mouth pressed against mine and this kiss came with a smile, a pair of them. And then it was all business. Serious, sensual, with his body pressed fully against mine. And if there had been a wall behind me, he would've pushed me back and held me against it. It was that kind of kiss and my heart pounded.

This time, he broke the kiss and stepped back. But then Viktor, who'd patiently—I guessed—waited for me to kiss the other two, spun me around, pulled me against him and laid a kiss on me that was so deep and so potent, a mash of mouths and a burning trail of hands, it was enough to carry me through at least for tonight. I hadn't been kissed in a while before I met—erm, re-met—Henryk, so this was intense but equally dreamy.

This sort of thing just didn't happen to me.

When he finally let me go, I let myself smile, feeling intoxicated. I'd just kissed all my husbands and it was divine. *Once we get to Spain*—and we were most definitely in Spain now—*it's no holds barred.* It was what we'd agreed on. What we'd all—except Henryk, anyway—had said.

When I took a tentative step away and no one opened a mouth to speak, I gave them a jaunty little finger wave. Then I turned and walked to the staircase that wrapped around the perimeter of the upstairs hall.

"Gentlemen, please try to work out your issues by morning. Or I'm going home." And that was all I had to say.

Erin

It certainly wasn't every day that I got kissed by—or kissed—three men. And definitely not kissed like *that*. Those weren't kisses for the timid or the faint of heart. Those hadn't been little nibbles or grazes. No accidental contact.

Now that I'd walked away, I was in my room freaking out about it.

I wasn't tired anymore, that was certain. I was wired, pacing from one corner of my room to the other. I probably could've summoned one or more of them up here to help me expend some of my wayward energy, but that would've been wrong.

I'd made my point, and now it was their call whether or not they were willing to make this vacation what it was meant to be. Otherwise, I'd have to do the most difficult thing I'd ever done, and actually go home.

I didn't want to leave them, but I would if I had to.

I looked at my cell. There were any number of social media sites I could've perused, could've made a dance video clip or two— I'd been known to rock it every once in a while—or I could sit on the bed and watch cat videos. Any of those things would have probably squelched my energy, but I wasn't in the mood for it.

Instead, I dialed Bree's number. She was six hours behind me, so she was probably just getting back to work from lunch. It was only one o'clock back home, and luckily for me, she picked up on the fifth ring.

"Girl!" It wasn't her customary greeting and there was quite an echo in the background. She must have been hiding in a bathroom to talk to me, which was good because the information I was about to impart was not for public consumption.

"I know!"

"You're in Ibiza!"

"I know!"

"And you're married to three guys? Are they hot? I mean on a

Pee-Wee Herman to Johnny Depp scale, where are they?" I'd only given her the basics and hadn't talked to her since I got off the plane in Lichtenstein and shot her a text.

"Young, beautiful Johnny. Every one of them." I smiled because he was her go-to fantasy guy. "Unfortunately, they're all acting like someone stole their favorite toy."

"Uh... what?"

Maybe the connection was bad?

"They hate each other," I tried to explain, though it wasn't quite that bad. "Well, two of them hate the other one and he hates them back." That was going to make the poly part of our relationship volatile, and I didn't care for it.

"Please tell me your resolution involves tossing them all in a mud-wrestling pit and you're planning to live-stream it."

I loved her for making me smile, but how was I going to explain that this was a real problem? *The pissing contest*, as Ray had so eloquently put it, was about to wreck my vacation and my proposed poly relationship.

"No. If they can't figure out their shit, I'm coming home." Sad as I was to say it.

"You're going to let a few bad attitudes ruin your free vacation?" Her tone was incredulous and it made me calm enough to finally sit down on the bed.

She had a point. But... "There was almost a fist fight."

"They were fighting over you?" She sounded excited and I was afraid she wasn't quite grasping the gravity of the situation.

I'd never been the kind of woman who enjoyed conflict. As a matter of fact, conflict made my stomach hurt. "There's nothing good about it."

"Unless you really can convince them to mud wrestle."

I laughed this time. "You're a one-track record today."

"And you have no idea how to take advantage of what's right in front of you." She laughed. "Have you even kissed any of your husbands?"

"All three of them. A few minutes ago," I admitted.

Bree waited, her silence demanding details—all the dirty details. I just knew it.

"It was... incredible."

"Is there one that's the best at it?"

I considered her question, remembering all three kisses and how they made me feel. "Nope. They're all different, that's for sure, but each one... *mmmm*." Each one gave me belly butterflies and woke up everything between my legs.

"Now, I'm jealous." She blew out so her lips made the motor sound. "Come on, Erin. Why are you holding out on me?"

"I'm not, it's just..." I didn't know how I felt about any of it. "They're all so..."

So, what? I couldn't find a word except *hostile* which wasn't really fair, because Silas and Viktor weren't hostile to one another. I lay back on the bed and looked up at the ceiling.

"Oh, come on."

"They all so... full of *testosterone*!"

Bree laughed. "You mean... virile?"

Oh, yeah. They were definitely that. "Yep. And handsome. And built. How am I supposed to resist all of that? Even if they hate each other, they don't hate me and maybe, if I stick it out, I can bring them around. Or maybe I'm just being full of myself?"

"Of course, you can bring them around." She laughed. "For goodness' sake, Erin. You're in Ibiza with three hot guys. Doesn't matter how you got there. It was fate or some weird destiny thing. Something right out of a movie plot."

Oh, yeah. Definitely a little bit Lifetime movie weird.

"Is there a point?" I hoped so. I needed a point to hang onto.

"Of course, there's a point." She chuckled. "I always have a point."

It just took a lot longer to get to it than I appreciated. This time I understood the frustration that generally resulted when someone who didn't know her very well got bogged down in her pauses and long breaths.

"Bree?"

"Oh, yeah. My point is that fate got you to Europe in this wonderful and slightly weird way. You can't thumb your nose at fate. She obviously wants you on this trip."

Oh. That was the point.

"I know." And I'd thought that, too. "But this is a lot of drama. And it turns out that boy drama is a lot worse than girl drama." It was a simple truth and one I hadn't realized before now. "Girl drama is all dirty looks and snide comments. Boy drama is all that, plus chest beating and dick measuring, fists flying—"

"Whoa, whoa, whoa. Back up. Anybody grabs a tape measure and you don't video that for me, our friendship is over." She cackled hard this time.

I couldn't help but laugh because she was acting like she didn't already have a parade of hot men walking through her house on their morning-after walks of shame.

"Fine. If there's a tape measure—"

"Or ruler." She wasn't going to let this go.

"Or ruler—"

"Or yardstick."

"If there is any type of measuring implement brought out, my phone camera will capture it and you'll be my first call." It was an easy promise to make.

"Good. And you, my friend, just stay on that rollercoaster and see where it ends." I could picture her grin in my head. "Trust the process. It'll be worth it, I promise!"

Of course, she was right. Bree was always right. She had intuition about men. Well, about the men I dated. She couldn't tell a dude from a dud when it came to her own love life.

"You win." Although, it seemed to me like I was probably the only one with anything at stake here. "I'll stay."

"Keep me posted, okay?" She paused. "And if you think about coming home before your vacation is over, you'll call me? I mean, if it really is that bad…"

I sighed. "I don't want to come home early, but I will if I have to. And of course I'll keep you posted."

But if these guys didn't figure out how to get along, there wasn't going to be anything to tell.

CHAPTER 15

Henryk

I twisted, tossed and turned. Then I counted sheep. I stared at the ceiling, watched an old telenovela on television, read the autobiography of an American president, and still I couldn't sleep.

Stress. Aggravation. The fact was that I couldn't stop thinking about Erin and that kiss. In my experience, women didn't kiss like that. But my experience was limited. I'd dated two women.

How pathetic was that? I was one of *From Your Lips* magazine's top one-hundred most influential people and I'd only kissed two women. Only had sex with one. More than one time, but still only the one woman.

That was not information I wanted to share with Erin or the other two. The same two who'd shared a woman before and were all about sharing Erin. *A poly relationship.* I didn't even know how such a thing was supposed to work.

My regular relationships—well, the one that actually counted as a relationship—had been a nightmare to work around. Between my parents, the paparazzi, an entire country watching me like I was about to topple off the pedestal they had put me on and worshipped, I always had eyes on me, someone watching, usually photographing. For all I knew, the hotel staff was earning tattletale money as I was supposed to have been sleeping.

Being a prince *looked* glamorous, and *seemed* like it was something out of a fairy tale. And this wasn't the poor little rich boy inside of me whining it out. This was truth. This was my life. And my future, the future of the entire country was riding on this.

That was a lot of pressure. And then when I factored in what I wanted, it was amazing I didn't walk with a hunchback from the weight of it all.

I walked down to the kitchen, looking for distraction, and found the Property Brothers sitting by the infinity pool drinking room service beers and eating take-out pizza. When I turned and started to walk back upstairs, one of them called out, "Hey, Prince Charming, come back. Have a beer."

Prince Charming beat Fancy Pants, which had to mean that our chat after Erin's threat must've been real, not just lip service. They were trying. And for me to prove I was too, I had to give them a chance.

I stared at the infinity pool for a few seconds, shrugged, then walked out onto the patio. Erin was worth trying this weird relationship for. I didn't know it for sure because I didn't know her very well. But I knew enough to know I couldn't stop thinking about her and that I was willing to do a whole lot of whatever she wanted. At least until someone found out and the whole thing blew up in my face.

"What's up? Thought you went to bed." Silas handed me a

beer from one of the six-packs and I sat on the edge of one of the lounge chairs.

"I did. Couldn't sleep."

"Yeah, it's a lot to think about," Silas said, then chuckled.

A guy like him wouldn't have a problem with this kind of thing. Hell, he *didn't* have a problem with it. It had been partly his idea.

"I can assure you, my friend, it's worth it. So worth it." He said it slow and with inflection. This was a man who believed what he said.

Viktor nodded. "Oh, yeah. Chicks mean maintenance. A lot of it. I mean, if you want them to be happy. Which we do. So, there's listening. Foot rubs, body massages."

Didn't sound horrible to me.

"It means making time, which can be hard around work and shit. Now, the way Si and I work it... I take baseball season. He's a huge baseball fan. He takes football season and we split hockey. I give shoulder massages and foot rubs. He cooks."

"I watch chick flicks and he takes her star-gazing." Silas grinned. "And at night, we take turns. Or we tag team. Or we work together to make sure no terrain is left untouched."

Terrain? Interesting, but understood.

"And the women like it that way?" From the way they spoke, it was like they had women lined up.

They both laughed.

"Hell, yeah. They love it. And they're grateful." Viktor nodded like he was speaking a secret, coded language. "*So* fucking grateful. I mean, everyone goes into it knowing what they're getting."

I nodded, my cock heavy. I could use a little grateful right now. Especially after that kiss from Erin.

"Haven't you ever thought about that?" Silas looked at me, eyebrows halfway up his forehead and one of those cocky smiles on his face.

Of course, I'd thought about this kind of thing. Prince or not, I was still a man. I just didn't talk much about it and I'd never thought I would have the opportunity. So, it was purely fantasy territory, for me. At least, it had been, until Viktor's invitation to join them on this trip.

"Women have fantasies too." Viktor nodded at his own statement. "They watch porn like the rest of us. They just don't advertise it."

"Porn? Are you... I mean..." I couldn't finish. The only woman I'd been with wouldn't have watched porn, I was sure of it.

"Yeah. There was this one chick..." Viktor rattled off a story of a past conquest, which was interesting enough.

But what they didn't seem to realize was that I didn't have the same freedoms they did. I couldn't just meet a random woman or two and take them to bed. Together. That would not remain a private thing. Every action of mine would be watched, and judged. That had been drilled into my head since I was young. I always had to be careful who I let close to me, who I let talk to me, who I was in a room beside. Or with.

I wanted to try and explain that to them.

"I can't just be with anyone I want, like you guys can. My dates are vetted by a security team, the woman investigated, my parents have their say, and then the public and their social media gets involved. It's treacherous to navigate." I could only imagine how badly this would turn out for all of us if the press got a hold of things. "If I'm with someone, the entire country and anyone with internet access and an interest in royal families knows about it."

I wasn't exaggerating. Once, I'd been followed through Lichtenstein by a woman who just wanted an autograph and ran my car off the road. I ended up with a broken arm and it could've been worse because my car rolled when she forced me onto a shoulder of the road and my driver lost control.

Guys like Silas and Viktor seemed to have it made. "You guys don't have to worry about judgmental parents who feel like it's their privilege or their responsibility—" Either way, the result was the same. "—to remind you that you're being watched for everything you do."

Silas nodded, looking thoughtful. "Yeah. I'm sure that'd be awful." He glanced at Viktor, then back at me. "But nobody knows you here."

He was wrong. "Someone will recognize me. I'm certain of it. As long as they have internet and cell phones, I can't be too careful." If Ray was still up, he'd tell them. He'd seen it all firsthand, even though he'd only worked for me for a few years.

"But you're allowed to have a vacation? To take a break?" Silas tilted his head like he was mid-idea.

"From my life and being who I am?" I shook my head. "I wish." It wasn't as if I could stop being a prince for the space of this week. I was high-profile and there was no way to hide from it.

"Maybe," Viktor said, seeming to be on the same wavelength as Silas. "You're getting married, so you're on one last vacation with a group of friends before you become a family man. Any photographers or paparazzi come calling, we're just a group of friends hanging out at the beach in Ibiza." He made it sound so easy.

"But at night, when it's just the four of us behind closed doors..." Silas was wearing that grin again.

"And Ray." Viktor was all about helping out.

"And Ray," Silas agreed. "Then you're just one of the guys dating a beautiful woman and taking her to the heights of what we all hope will be sexual euphoria."

Silas did make it sound euphoric. And easy.

"If this ever comes out..." There wouldn't be an expanse of space large enough for me to put between me and my parents.

"It won't. Just play it cool," Viktor said, a grin plastered all over his face.

"Yeah. No worries. We've got your back, Prince Charming." Silas handed me another beer. And for the first time in a very long time, I relaxed enough to consider all this.

It was a lot to wager, a lot to lose. But even if it all came out, I'd be forgiven the moment my engagement was announced, surely? It would never be forgotten of course, but did I not have the right to a single week of freedom before my nuptials?

"All right. I'm in."

I'd never thought I'd be able to love a woman like Erin. I had definitely never considered a poly arrangement, where I would be sharing a woman with two other men. But now, being with her was a burning need, a soul desire. And come hell or high water, I was going to find a way to make it happen.

Viktor

It was impossible not to think about Erin, not to want her, not to imagine all the different things I wanted to do to her body that made my dick twitch. But when she stripped down to a bikini, put on a wide-brimmed hat and lay back on a chaise in the sand to sunbathe, I almost swallowed my tongue. My cock was one throb from peeking out the top of my shorts.

She was luscious. Curved. The woman had a body that made me want to plunge inside of her, ram my cock home into her beautiful channel...

A hard-on while riding a rented jet ski was not the ideal situation. But I couldn't stop the rush of thoughts about Erin. They were the reason I spent most of the day semi-hard. I was sure Silas was equally afflicted. From where we were riding not far offshore, we could see the beach, and see her lying there, glistening with suntan oil.

Fuck. She was an eyeful. And as a man with eyes, I was grateful.

She stood up and used her hat to fan herself. Then she stretched, and my mouth went dry. She was all lines and curves and I wanted to lick and kiss every inch of her.

Silas pulled up beside my wave runner, and we both stared at her. And then there were three, as Henryk pulled up, too.

"How the fuck is anyone supposed to resist that?" Si pointed at the beach. Then suddenly, like she could hear us, she looked out at the water and waved. "Honestly. Holy shit."

"I sure as hell don't plan on resisting anything." No point in pretending. I wanted her, and after that kiss last night, no way could she say that she wasn't into the idea. She'd kissed each one of us and she'd done it with passion and precision. She'd done it with conviction. She'd done it, to show all three of us, that she was into it. Equally. If we could get our shit together and stop fighting.

My cock swelled again just thinking about that kiss.

I turned the jet ski out of our little trio and rode farther from the shore before I embarrassed myself. Or before I went back to the beach and hauled her against me.

We spent the day on the water, stealing glances at her while she sunbathed and read and waded into the surf to cool off. Those minutes were the best minutes of the day.

Turned out, Henryk wasn't so much a stuffy prince as he was just a guy who needed to get out more. And he knew how to ride a jet ski. How to fish. Probably could walk on water if he put his mind to it.

By afternoon, we put our toys away and walked onto the beach. The sand was white and hot beneath our feet, but worth every second to get closer to Erin. I moved to stand beside the chaise where Erin, who had a collection of empty cocktail glasses on the table next to her, was sunbathing topless now. Although we couldn't see anything naughty yet, since she was lying on her belly.

Silas seized the day, because he was confident enough to do that kind of thing. He poured a dollop of honey-colored suntan oil onto his hands, sat beside her, then rubbed it onto her back. Her smooth, supple skin already shone a golden brown. Everywhere his hand swiped, he left a shimmering trail of glitter-infused oil. She shifted a little, widening her legs to the edges of the chaise. The view was incredible.

Erin moaned as Silas's hands skimmed across her lower back, and his little finger dipped into the waistband of her bikini bottoms, trailing along the delicious curve of her ass.

My mouth watered as his finger veered lower and she swirled

her hips. He leaned in and whispered, but not quite low enough to avoid Henryk and me hearing, "Turn over and I'll do your front." And then he kissed her shoulder and moved his hand further beneath her bikini bottoms.

She moaned again and shifted some more, using her body to encourage his hand lower, closer to her pussy. "Mmm."

I sat on the chaise next to hers and took the bottle of oil, poured some into my hand and then began to massage it into one of her thighs. I'd jerked off last night, imagining how soft her skin would be, but the reality was better than my imagination. So much better.

I kneaded her skin, stroking along the muscle. Then I let my hand move higher, let my fingers do the walking, slipping inside the elastic riding high on her ass cheek. Certainly, it was my plan to also move closer to her hot spot.

I nodded to Henryk, who was watching with a hungry look in his eyes. She had another leg and we had plenty of lotion. No reason the prince shouldn't join in and have a little fun too. Erin was obviously into it, so why not?

But he shook his head and sat on a neighboring chaise, simply watching. When I squeezed her ass, she sighed, lifted her hips, and pushed herself into our hands. Silas cupped her ass low, his fingers close to the promised land.

"Excuse me, Your Highness?" The voice was startling when I was concentrating so hard on Erin's contented sighs and her tiny moans of pleasure.

I jerked away from Erin. Silas pulled his hand out, and we all looked up at Ray. Erin was still on her belly, but she turned to shield her eyes from the sun and see what was happening.

To his credit, Ray didn't act as if there was anything amiss in finding Erin mostly naked with us all fawning over her. He looked at Henryk. "There's a helicopter circling above, sir. We should get you inside before you're tomorrow's headline."

Henryk nodded and allowed Ray to usher him up the beach to the patio and into the common area of our suite. Erin jumped up and wrapped herself in a towel then hurried after them. Silas and I stayed behind for a few minutes.

"Fucking helicopter." Silas looked up, flipping it off as it hovered not far from the shore. Far enough a telephoto lens would've likely still be blurry, but not so far as to mistake the gesture Silas made. It was universal.

"Right?" He'd been ready to go knuckle deep, and I hadn't been far behind him. Dammit. She'd been warm and ready. Maybe we should've moved her inside, reaping the rewards of our efforts. But instead, we were on the beach and Henryk had her all to himself. The letdown was real.

I flopped onto Erin's lounger and wished I had a beer. I looked over at Silas, who was also reclined on the lounger Henryk had vacated. "So, what do you think about Prince Charming in there?"

He shrugged. "Don't know. I don't think he's ever going to be as relaxed out of the water as he was on it."

True. He'd only watched us then, not touched her. But I'd seen the need in his eyes. Even last night when she kissed him, he hadn't done much more than lay a hand at the small of her back, but the desire when he looked at Erin was unmistakable. This might be too much for him.

"But he wants her," I said, shaking my head. Why couldn't he just be like me or Silas, and admit his feelings for her? "Even somebody as uptight as he is can't disguise a boner when he's wearing swim shorts."

Silas chuckled. "Wanting her might not be enough. I mean if he was..."

"Normal?" It was easy to figure out where Silas's mind was at. Even if I didn't know him so well and he wasn't like a brother to me, I'd know what he meant because I thought the same thing.

Silas nodded. "Yeah." He paused and looked out at the water. "Even if we somehow manage to make a poly out of this with him, it can't last."

"Obviously. The guy's a prince. And they found him here already." I pointed to the empty sky as if the helicopter hadn't flown away once Henryk left the beach. "There's no way to make this long-term."

He nodded. As usual, we were on the same page. And then he grinned. "But this is our vacation with her, and I'm thinking that so long as we keep her happy, she'll keep us happy." His smile widened. "And, whether Prince Charming goes all in or not, I think *we* know how to keep a woman like Erin happy."

"We do." So true.

That sounded good to me. So fucking good.

CHAPTER 16

Erin

When we left the beach, I immediately went to my room. I showered because I had a coating of oil so thick on my body, if one of them had decided to get on top of me, he would have slid right off.

There were about thirty different ways I wanted them to have me. All of them. That was a given. I hadn't been able to think about much else since we got here. The agreement we'd made in Lichtenstein was never far from my mind and I'd found it hard to think about much else. The deal was, we would wait until we were on the island. And now we were *on the island*.

Not that I wasn't anxious. I'd never done something like this before. Sex, yes. Three men at one time? No. It was unnerving just to think of it.

Unnerving, but so exciting.

Tonight, we were going out. Dinner. Dancing. Drinking. The whole nine yards.

It was about half past seven when the dress arrived at my

room, courtesy of Henryk, of course. And this thing was stunning. Silver and sparkly, short, backless. One wrong move, and my wardrobe malfunction would be catastrophic.

Although, that might've been the point. I pulled on a pair of strappy stilettos and walked down to the common area.

And *hello*. Henryk was in a soft cashmere sweater the same shade as his eyes and gray slacks. Silas wore jeans and a button down that made his chest look broader and his legs longer. Victor wore a black t-shirt with jeans. Never before had I ever been so grateful for a t-shirt, but this one was tight and stretched across his defined pecs.

My belly quivered in anticipation and my breath caught in my throat. It was going to be a long and hopefully fulfilling night.

Silas smiled when he saw me, then Henryk and Viktor ceased whatever they'd been chatting about and gaped at me. So, this silver dress was already worth its weight in, well, silver. I smiled back at them all, suddenly feeling like a million dollars under the scrutiny of three lustful sets of eyes.

Ray walked in behind me and leaned in to whisper, "Get 'em, girl."

I grinned at him over my shoulder. "Oh, I plan to." And I meant it. Every single one of them.

We were having dinner at Calma, a restaurant with a port-view terrace. Silas took my hand as we walked from the hotel to the waiting car and I loved being able to lean into his strength. Feel his heat against me.

It was about twenty minutes to the restaurant and I sat in the back between Victor and Silas while Henryk sat in the front with Ray, who was driving.

Every once in a while, Henryk would glance behind him and

catch my eye. I finally timed my wink right and he grinned involuntarily when he saw me before he turned back to face the front.

It was in that moment that Viktor slid his work-roughened palm from my knee up to my mid-thigh. He lowered his head to whisper, "Your skin is like silk. Beautiful."

I could really grow to like a man who knew how to use his words. And I would've told him that too, if not for Silas, who at that moment slid one of the straps from my shoulder and pressed his lips to where it had been.

I would've been able to breathe fine, too, had he not flicked his tongue out to swirl the flesh there. I gasped and Viktor's hand moved up my thigh to the edge of my panties.

Instead of hiking the short skirt of my dress even higher, I clamped my legs together, which trapped Viktor's hand between my legs. But when I twisted toward him, the side of my dress Silas had loosened fell away. I now had one exposed breast.

Before I could react and pull the dress back up, Silas's palm covered my nipple, and I gasped from surprise and pleasure. When we hit a bump in the road, the friction of his palm on my sensitized flesh was delicious. But we were in a car. And as beautiful as all the sensations were, it was a bit too public for such wanton behavior.

"Let's eat dinner first," I managed, albeit in a breathless fashion.

They grunted assent, so I set Viktor's hand free and tucked my breast away. Ray smiled at me in the rear-view mirror. He pulled the car up in front of the restaurant and stopped.

"Oh good, we're here," I said, amidst amused smiles from Viktor and Silas. They were a formidable team, and I had the feeling that once they got me somewhere safe, I'd learn the full meaning of *no holds barred*.

And I couldn't wait!

We all hopped out of the car, me on wobbly legs. Damn, those boys were good at seduction! Henryk handed the keys to the valet and we walked in.

There was no fanfare of flashing cameras, thank goodness, and after a few minutes of surreptitious glancing around, Henryk relaxed as much as I thought he could. He sat beside me at the table and Silas and Viktor sat together on the other side. I didn't know where Ray had gone, but I assumed he was nearby and watching, just in case of trouble.

Henryk spoke to the waiter in perfect Spanish, and I smiled at how awesome he sounded. In fact, I might've swooned a little had I not already been sitting. He made the language sound so romantic, so sensual. If I didn't know better, I would've thought he was asking the waiter to come back to the hotel with us. But the waiter left and then returned a couple of minutes later with a bottle of wine.

When I laid my hand on the table, Henryk covered it with his own. He gave mine a quick squeeze then pulled away, as if he craved the touch but didn't quite have the courage to go for it. I knew why he did it like that, of course, but I wanted so much more. I wanted to touch and be touched. Properly.

I placed my hand on his leg, and stroked his thigh lightly with my fingers. I was already on edge from the car ride, dealing with swirling need not just in my belly and between my legs but everywhere in my body. I wanted dinner over already, so we could get to the club and start dancing. There was nothing I wanted more than the three hot bodies I was at the table with to grind and gyrate in time with mine.

But first, I had to get through the meal.

"You look beautiful tonight, Erin." That was Viktor, always ready with a compliment.

I smiled at him. "Thank you. You all look nice, too." Nice wasn't accurate. They looked incredible. Amazing. Hot as fuck. But everything I tried to come up with in my head seemed too bland, so I didn't bother amending what I'd said.

"I think we should toast to what a wonderful night this is going to be. I'm grateful you all stopped the bickering today." I lifted my glass. "And let's toast how lucky I am to be here with all of you." Another understatement, but I didn't know another word for lucky.

The guys had really pulled it together for me today. They'd been perfect. No fighting. No death daggers, at least that I knew of. They'd played like kids in the water, zooming around on jet skis like old friends.

The fear that I'd carried with me all last night, that I might have to leave, was now gone. We were all on the same page. *I think.*

Henryk smiled in response and I gave his leg a gentle squeeze. He really was beautiful—they all were. And that wasn't the wine talking, I hadn't even had a sip yet. It was a simple fact, undeniable to anyone who saw them.

"I think we're the lucky ones, but I can drink to what a wonderful night this is. And what a wonderful night it's going to be." Viktor pulled his lower lip between his teeth, and he looked almost boyish.

But then his words registered properly and I saw his eyes, dark with want and desire. An involuntary shiver worked its way down my spine.

As I stared back at him, Henryk shifted closer to me and I got a big whiff of his deliciously spicy cologne. When I tilted my head, I could feel the warmth of him on my cheek, and I loved it.

Perhaps I shouldn't have been so into this, but I liked him. I liked all of them. Maybe too much. Because this had to be a crazy idea. I'd risked my job to take this vacation with them. But there was no regret in me. Nothing that said I shouldn't be doing this.

I could barely eat, but it wasn't anxiety that stopped my appetite for food. It wasn't apprehension. It was something different. Something good.

Anticipation. It had been a long time since I had anything to look forward to as much as I was looking forward to what was coming later tonight.

I finished my glass of wine because I needed to calm down and I thought the alcohol would help, but the more I drank, the more the lines blurred.

By the time we arrived at the club and headed onto the dance floor, my body was on fire for them.

The heavy thump and beat of the music made every primal instinct inside of me rear its head. I danced with all of them at the same time. Silas gyrated behind me with his cock hard against my ass. Viktor stood in front of me, his hips aligned with mine. Henryk was right beside us, his hands grazing my arm and the curve of my hip. Every grind, every thrust, every touch, was a prelude to what they wanted. What we all wanted.

Then they shifted positions and Silas was in front of me and Henryk slid in behind me, until Viktor slid him around a little so each of them could claim one of my hips. Henryk leaned down and kissed my throat, and I turned my face to let him kiss my mouth.

Instead of turning away, as I half feared he might, he held me by the face and deepened our kiss. He slid his tongue between my lips and pulled me against him. I threaded my fingers into his hair and held onto him while he kissed me not just with his lips, but with his entire body.

One of his hands slid from my face down my form to my ass. He yanked me closer and aligned our bodies. He groaned, and an answering moan rasped from my lips. My pussy was pulsing and my nipples were hard. How much longer until we went home?

Silas whispered in my ear, "Let's get out of here, gorgeous girl."

Oh, yeah.

I was so ready, I could barely stand. My legs trembled with the need to fulfil this ache inside of me. In the history of ready, no one was more ready than I was. Right. This. Minute.

I pulled back from my passionate kiss with Henryk and walked somewhat unsteadily off the dance floor. The boys followed and I waited at the door for Ray to get the car as the others came up behind me. We hadn't lasted but one dance and I wanted them so badly.

Wanted to kiss and be kissed, touch and be touched, until they were trembling with the same level of need that was already pulsing through me.

In the car, I sat between Henryk and Viktor this time, while Silas reluctantly rode up front. I kissed Viktor, enjoying his taste and soft moans. Then I turned to kiss Henryk again. Viktor kissed the nape of my neck while Henryk ravaged my mouth. Silas turned in his seat and leaned through the gap to run his hand over my thigh, pushing my legs apart.

Every sensation was more intense than the last, better than the one before it. I never wanted it to end. The car rolled to a stop and Henryk pulled away as if he expected someone to be waiting for us when we got out of the car.

But Viktor and I climbed out together into the cool night air, and I wasn't even tipsy anymore. Silas joined us a few seconds later. There were going to be no excuses tomorrow. In the morning we were going to be happy about what happened tonight, without any regrets, knowing we'd made this decision without the aid of alcohol.

Henryk didn't get out of the car. I leaned down and looked in at him. "Come on."

At his stricken look, my heart began to pound. "Aren't you coming?"

He paused, staring at me with all the intensity of a man about to make a life-changing decision. He still wore my lipstick on his mouth. But instead of getting out of the car, he shook his head. "I can't. If anyone ever found out... my name would never recover and my parents..." He shook his head again. "I can't. But you can. You can be with them, and you should. It's what you want. They're good guys, Erin. And they like you a lot."

"I want them. But I want you too, Henryk."

He smiled softly but there was no changing this guy's mind. That was obvious. Even so...

"Please?" I asked, extending my hand to touch him again. I had to try.

He shook his head and slid further away along the seat.

"Okay. If you change your mind, you know where to find us."

I stepped back and Henryk pulled the door shut. Sadness pushed through me. Despite all my hopes and plans and our beautiful kisses, he wouldn't be joining us after all.

Ray slowly drove away, and I watched them go, not knowing where they were going, or what to say to the others. None of us knew the pressure Henryk had to deal with, and I'd probably never really understand. I didn't want to. But I had hoped he could get past some of his hang-ups, at least for tonight.

I turned to Silas and Viktor. We could go into the common area or take the elevator up to the second-floor rooms. I loved the set-up of this place. So many options.

As sad as I was to see Henryk driven away, I still had two wonderfully hot and sexy guys ready for me right here.

"Shall we?" I asked, and sashayed through the doors into the common area, then over to hit the second-floor button. The elevator was moving way too slow for me now. I turned to Silas and kissed him, then twisted out of his kiss and pressed my mouth to Viktor's.

With two of my men taking it in turns to kiss me, I didn't care how slowly the elevator moved, or if it stopped, or if the bottom fell out of it.

When the door finally dinged open, I tugged my stiletto shoes off my aching feet and held them in my left hand. We then walked down the hallway—jogged, actually—to the door to my suite. I pulled the key out of my bag and handed it to Silas as Viktor used his body to hold me against the wall in a kiss that was as passionate as it was sensual.

He guided me inside the room without breaking the kiss, the door closing behind us. Then Viktor turned me so that I could kiss the impatiently-waiting Silas. Viktor's hands skimmed my sides, from the hem of my revealing dress upward. His thumbs brushed my sensitive nipples through the dress and pleasure exploded inside me.

I broke off from the kiss to pant, "Oh my God, that feels so good."

"We're only just beginning," Viktor said as he slid the straps of the dress from my shoulders and kissed one shoulder blade, then the other.

Silas continued to kiss me like he was a man dying of thirst in the desert and I was his oasis. I couldn't get enough of the feeling of being so wanted, so desired.

I had one hand tangled in Silas's hair and the other twisted behind me to grip Viktor's t-shirt and hold him against my body. My hand shifted lower, finding Viktor's rock-hard ass, almost as hard as the cock he had pressed against me. He slid his hand along the arm I had around Silas and moved it down. I let him position me however he wanted, trusting him to look after me.

Then he moved both straps down so that the dress slithered down my body and pooled at my feet.

I was standing in a pair of panties and nothing else, exposed to them. I didn't feel vulnerable though. I felt safe. Cherished, even.

While Silas continued to kiss my lips, Viktor fondled one of my breasts with one hand and slid down my stomach with his other. Then he moved even lower and anticipation arced through me.

I wanted to feel their skin, the brush of fine chest hair against my breasts. My fingers fumbled with the buttons on Silas's shirt while Viktor continued toying with my nipple. With his other hand edging into my panties, he was almost touching my clit.

I was throbbing so badly. Aching, deep in my pussy for them.

Silas broke our kiss, then they were each kissing my neck and I pushed his shirt down his arms. Then Silas's skin was against mine. God, it felt even better than I'd imagined. Warm and silky-smooth. Hard underneath, and yet with a silken surface that heated my own skin ten-fold.

Victor turned my head to cup my jaw so I could kiss him. Silas bent to take a nipple into his mouth, between his teeth, gently, lightly. My head fell back again and Viktor finally pushed his hand down with a little bit of pressure and found my ready core.

When his finger dipped inside of me, my knees buckled. He whispered something unintelligible in my ear and I sighed. This was perfect.

For me, the Never-Have-I-Ever game just got a lot more interesting.

My hands were remarkably empty. This time, when I reached behind me, I laid my hand over Viktor's zipper. I could feel his flesh, long and thick. Gloriously hard. I gave him a gentle squeeze then a firmer one, running my palm up and down a few times. He stopped kissing me to groan against my throat.

Silas dragged a trail of hot, wet kisses down my body until I felt his breath and then his tongue against the inside of my thigh. He pulled his head back and looked up at me. "Time for you to get on the bed, Erin."

That wasn't something I had to be told twice. But instead of waiting for me to move, Silas stood and lifted me into his arms. Then he turned and put me on the bed.

I wriggled up the mattress and lay down, my chest heaving with my breathing. I'd never been so turned on before. When I finally had my head on the pillow and was flat on my back, the boys came to lie down next to me, one on each side.

Viktor kissed one tight, aching nipple and Silas flicked the other with his tongue. Someone slid a finger inside of me, making me cry out and clamp my legs together. I was so close to coming. But I wanted more.

My back arched up. "I'm the only one undressed." My words were breathless, and I sounded wanton, even to my own ears, but I needed them naked beside me. Viktor got up and undressed quickly, then slid his body back down next to mine.

"Let me taste you," I begged. I didn't know the etiquette for this type of interlude, if there even was such a thing, but I wasn't afraid to ask for what I wanted.

He moved to kneel beside me so that I only had to turn my head to take him into my mouth. He was hot, hard, and slightly salty. Perfect in every way.

I curled my fingers around the thickness of his shaft and stroked his cock while I licked and sucked on the head. He groaned, deep and loud.

Silas had moved between my thighs, his hands pushing my legs apart. I welcomed the touch, opening wide for him. "Ohhh... Ahhh..." My moans were muted around Viktor's cock as Silas kissed my pussy, then began to eat me.

I writhed and shifted under his expert mouth, moaning and gasping with pleasure. Silas slid his hands under me and grabbed my ass, lifting my pussy to better access it. He teased my clit with flicks of his tongue and coaxed my body to tighten with every kiss.

I was coiled, ready to spiral out of control. Silas moaned against my clit as his tongue ravaged me. The pressure was building, and suddenly it was too much.

I pulled my mouth off Viktor's cock, still stroking him hard.

"Please, Silas, fuck me." I wanted to feel him inside me when my body shattered, wanted this entire experience.

Silas rolled on a condom and knelt between my thighs. He grabbed me by the ass and pulled me up, impaling me on his cock.

I cried out at the pleasure. The exquisite torture of being filled to the brim. He pulled back, then thrust inside me again, deep, hard, and powerful. I turned my head, sobbing from the pleasure, and wrapped my lips around Viktor once more. I wanted both of them to pleasure me, at the same time. I wanted Silas to split me apart with his hard thrusting, and I wanted to feel Viktor swell in my mouth until he was ready to explode.

Silas rode me harder, faster, making my pussy tighten and peak in pleasure waves for him. I was going to come, and soon. With every thrust, he pushed me higher and higher.

When my orgasm finally hit like a massive wave crashing against the shore, I cried out around Viktor's cock. He pulled out and exploded against my throat with a groan as my body split apart from the pleasure of riding Silas's hard flesh.

My orgasm went on and on, my pussy milking Silas's cock as my belly trembled and shook. A moment later, Silas thrust deep inside me with a strangled moan and then his whole body stiffened and jerked as he reached his own pinnacle.

Every sound, every touch, every breath was etched into my memory. This was the most perfect night of my life. And the best part was, it was only the beginning.

CHAPTER 17

Henryk

I was on the outside, looking in. Not literally, because there was no way I'd be able to watch Erin having sex with Viktor and Silas without jumping in. I didn't like the feeling. At all. Not that it wasn't a trend in my life. My entire existence since I was born was that of someone always looking in from the periphery but never a part of the action.

Was that enough? I wanted it to be; wished it was enough. But deep down inside me there was a gaping hole that felt like it could never be filled, and that gave me my answer. It wasn't enough, just to observe as everyone else lived their lives to the full. Nowhere near it, but there wasn't much I could do about that.

I couldn't hear them, thank God. They were in her suite. Together. I was sitting down here on the beach with Ray, on twin loungers. We watched the water roll gently onto the sand, over and over, and all I could think about was what was going on inside. I wished with all my heart that I was in there with her. With them.

"What's wrong with you?" Ray asked, staring at me over his

bottle, his beer poised for a sip.

"Nothing."

He laughed and I rolled my eyes. I knew what was coming next from him—some witty observation about my mood and the overall *vibe* I was projecting.

"Sounds like you're trying to summon a dust storm with all that sighing." He smiled like he was Shakespeare, creating an image with his words.

"That's the best you can do?" I groaned. "I just gave up the chance of a lifetime. I should be in there sowing my wild oats before I give up my life to God and country and a woman who would never dream of participating in a three—no, *four*some. Or do you just want me to pass you another beer?"

He threw back his head and cackled. "Yes." I reached down into the ice chest beside me to get him a beer. "To all of it."

When I handed him the bottle, he smiled and twisted off the top.

"You gave up the opportunity of a lifetime," he said. "Erin is one in a billion and you know it. You *should* be in there sowing your wild oats before you marry what's-her-name. A woman, by the way, who is never going to let you bring anyone but her into your bedroom." He lifted his glass. "And thank you for the beer."

He was right. Of course, he was. He was always right, and it did me absolutely no fucking good. I would have much preferred he shut the hell up and let me lament my loss without his commentary. Especially plagiarized commentary I had just spoon-fed him.

I sat silently, hoping the sound of the waves would lull me into some semblance of peace. I waited, but it didn't work. My stomach felt all churned up and my head ached from all the images tumbling around inside it. Sensual images, of Erin being pleasured by Vik and Si, moaning her need and arching up as they gave her exactly what she wanted.

I let out a groan. "You can head inside, Ray. I'll be fine."

I had the moon and the waves and a few more beers to get through. There was even a light breeze that might cool my burning desire. *Yeah, right.*

He stood. "I know that you want to do what's best for the monarchy and for Lichtenstein, Henryk."

I looked up at him and nodded because he was right. I absolutely wanted to do what was best for my country and my family. The problem was, I had no idea what that was or how to make it happen.

I also had no idea how my wants and needs fit into that equation, or even *if* they did.

"Well, Your Highness," Ray said, reverting suddenly to the more formal address. "Who says that marrying that woman is what's best?"

And like Ray always did when he'd imparted a nugget of wisdom, he walked away, into the hotel, and let me ruminate alone on what he'd just said.

I stayed out all night, until the sunrise began to streak the sky in ambers and oranges. Then I dragged myself off the beach lounger with all my empty beer bottles and went to my suite. I slept fitfully until Erin knocked on the door and came in to sit beside me on the bed.

I yawned and sat up, scrubbing my hands over my face. I felt rugged and unfit for company. But Erin wasn't just company. She was smiling, and made the room brighter just by her very presence. "Morning."

I studied her intently, looking for something different in her demeanor after the night she must have had. But she just looked as vibrant and full of positive energy as ever.

"I missed you last night," she said softly, and then lifted my hand to thread her fingers with mine.

Erin was beautiful. Her eyes, the shine of her hair, the smile. She was also graceful and elegant. Kind and sincere. She was everything a woman should be and her sexy body was just a bonus. I still couldn't believe I'd passed up the chance to be with her, to see her thrashing and writhing with passion.

My cock began to harden at the thought.

"I can't." My voice was almost a groan. I cleared my throat, aiming for calm. "Lichtenstein is counting on me."

She scooted closer. "I didn't invite Lichtenstein into my room last night. I invited you." She leaned in and kissed my cheek then stood. "At least come out and eat breakfast with us. It's late, but we all overslept."

And there it was. That shy yet sensual grin as she clearly recalled the memories of last night. Memories that I hadn't been a part of. "I wish I could've been there too, Erin." There was no going back now. No way to undo my no-show. "I'll join you for breakfast," I added quickly. At least I could do that for her. "Thank you for asking."

After shooting me another quick smile, she walked out and shut the door behind her. I showered and dressed for the day even though all I wanted to do was crawl back into bed and start another fantastic dream about Erin.

By the time I walked down to the common area and sat beside Silas at the table, breakfast had already been served. Erin had one foot up on her chair and she was tearing a bagel into pieces, while

Viktor and Silas ate platefuls of eggs and bacon and even pancakes.

I ate fresh fruit—guava, mango and melon—and drank coffee.

Erin leaned over to feed me a strawberry from across the table, and giggled when I sucked her finger into my mouth. She smiled; purred, even.

Silas cleared his throat and Viktor nodded at me. "So, we have six days left."

"I'm aware." I didn't know if he wanted a calendar countdown or what the purpose was of reminding me how little time I had left with her.

He laughed. "Touchy."

Wouldn't you be? I nearly retorted, but swallowed it back. No doubt I was touchy, but I didn't like thinking about what was going to happen after our week was up. I sure as hell didn't want anyone pointing out to me how soon I would lose her altogether.

"Yes. I am," I admitted, after a long silence. "But if you understood what my life is about to become..."

I stopped. Now I sounded like a spoiled rich boy who didn't want to go home to his mansion. And it was true. I didn't want to go home to the castle or the woman who would soon be there waiting to marry me.

"Why does it have to be something you don't want?"

Because my future doesn't include Erin.

I didn't say the words aloud. Silas didn't understand, but I couldn't blame him.

"And even if it does have to be that way, why can't you just enjoy the time you have here?" Viktor nodded like he'd just found the solution to world peace. "Just let go. You're not the crown prince here."

It didn't matter how many times they said it, it was never going to be true. I *was* the crown prince of Lichtenstein, no matter what country I happened to be staying in. And there would always be people looking at me, watching me, waiting for me to be the disgrace other royals had proven to be. I couldn't do that to my family, or to my father. He was counting on me to step up and be responsible.

"Tell him." Silas looked at Erin.

She held out her hand and I lay mine on top of hers, giving a little squeeze. "Yes, do tell me, Erin."

If for no other reason so I could hear her voice before I packed my bags and headed home. I'd made the decision last night on the beach that I wouldn't stay the whole time. It would be too painful to go to bed alone every night while they did God knows what in theirs, just down the hallway.

I hadn't told them of my decision yet, and with her hand in mine, I wasn't itching to say it now.

She smiled and, as always, the room was brighter for it. "We have six days, Henryk."

It was getting painful to keep hearing it.

"And I don't want to waste whatever time you can spare me in those six days. Even if you can only give me the days, not the nights. Even if you can only give me an hour here or there. I want you here, Henryk. With us. On this vacation where anything is possible."

She pushed her chair back and walked around to stand beside me. I repositioned myself so that she could sit on my lap and when she did, it felt just right. I put my arms around her.

Erin went on. "I know you're worried about peeping Toms and photographers getting rich off your name and catching you in a compromising situation. But we will do our best not to let that happen."

Silas nodded. "That's right. We're going to make sure that what happens in Ibiza, stays in Ibiza."

Ray, who'd been silently watching television in the corner of the room—he'd become quite addicted to telenovelas—looked up. "You know, if you take this love festival back to Lichtenstein, Erin, this wouldn't be a problem." He shot a look at me. "What happens behind palace doors is your business, Your Highness."

He added a sarcastic bow at the end, but that was just Ray, and I was used to his insolence in the name of friendship.

"Makes for a good Plan B," Silas said, looking at me like what I was going to do mattered in the grand vacation scheme. But we all knew that, if I left for home, they would stay and continue having a good time without me. Wouldn't they?

"What do you say, pal?" Silas asked, and as if he already knew of my intent to leave, he added, "We'd like it if you stayed."

Viktor grunted. "It would make Erin very happy if you stayed, Prince Charming, and that makes me and Si happy, too."

I looked at all of them staring at me—Erin, Viktor, Silas, and even Ray. Maybe what I chose did matter to these people.

Something shifted in my chest at that realization. *They really want me here.*

A warmth spread through me, relaxing my tense muscles, and I began to stroke up and down on Erin's hips. She felt glorious, astride my lap, smiling down at me as if she cared.

She does care. She wants me to be part of this. How can I possibly leave her?

My hands on her curvy flesh tightened, as if my own body was trying to prove to me I couldn't leave. If I did, I'd regret it forever.

I might never get a chance to be with Erin again. I might never even *see* her again. The papers were signed, and the marriage dissolved. After this week, or the next or the one after, we would all return to our lives, to the obligations and responsibilities and the people counting on us. I wouldn't get another opportunity for happiness like this. Perhaps ever.

"A week." The words popped out of my mouth, and as they did, a sense of freedom filled me all the way up. Erin jiggled on my lap, laughing, and Silas slapped Viktor on the back.

I glanced at Ray and saw a satisfied smirk decorate his face.

"And then we can see," I added, feeling brave. "Maybe France or London. Or maybe even Lichtenstein."

I don't know how it had happened, but in the space of a few minutes, with a few sentences, my plans to leave had been flipped on their head.

One thing was for certain. There was no way I was going home now. Not without them. And if, after this week, we wanted more, then I would just have to convince them all that it was the right thing.

To return home to my palace. To the stress, the obligation and the prying eyes.

Heaven help me.

THE END of part 1.

* * *

Continued on in 'Vacation with Three Boys':
HEREhttps://geni.us/vacationthreeboys